I am the cheese

I am the cheese

A NOVEL BY

Robert Cormier

PANTHEON BOOKS

Copyright © 1977 by Robert Cormier
All rights reserved under
International and Pan-American Copyright Conventions.
Published in the United States by
Pantheon Books, a division of Random House, Inc.,
and simultaneously in Canada by
Random House of Canada Limited, Toronto.
Library of Congress Cataloging in Publication Data
Cormier, Robert. I am the cheese.

SUMMARY:

A young boy desperately tries to
unlock his past yet knows he must hide those
memories if he is to remain alive.
[1. Intelligence service—Fiction.
2. Organized crime—Fiction] I. Title.
PZ7.C81634Iac [Fic] 76-55948 ISBN 0-394-83462-3
Manufactured in the United States of America
10 9 8 7 6 5 4 3 2 1

I am the cheese is a
work of fiction. All names, characters,
and events are fictional, and any resemblance
to real persons or actual events
is unintentional.

For Chris,
my daughter.
With love.

I am the cheese

I am riding the bicycle and I am on Route 31 in Monument, Massachusetts, on my way to Rutterburg, Vermont, and I'm pedaling furiously because this is an old-fashioned bike, no speeds, no fenders, only the warped tires and the brakes that don't always work and the handlebars with cracked rubber grips to steer with. A plain bike—the kind my father rode as a kid years ago. It's cold as I pedal along, the wind like a snake slithering up my sleeves and into my jacket and my pants legs, too. But I keep pedaling, I keep pedaling.

This is Mechanic Street in Monument, and to my right, high above on a hill, there's a hospital and I glance up at the place and I think of my father in Rutterburg, Vermont, and my pedaling accelerates. It's ten o'clock in the morning and it is October, not a Thomas Wolfe October of burning leaves and ghost winds but a rotten October, dreary, cold, and damp with little sun and no warmth at all. Nobody reads Thomas Wolfe anymore, I guess, except my father and me. I did a book report on *The Web and the Rock* and Mr. Parker in English II regarded me with suspicion and gave me a *B–* instead of the usual *A*. But Mr. Parker and the school and all of that are behind me now and I pedal. Your legs do all the work on an old bike like this, but my legs feel good, strong, with staying power. I pass by a house with a white picket fence and I spot a little kid who's standing on the sidewalk and he watches me go by and I wave to him because he looks lonesome and he waves back.

I look over my shoulder but there's no one following.

At home, I didn't wave goodbye to anybody. I just left. Without fanfare. I didn't go to school. I didn't call anyone. I thought of Amy but I didn't call her. I woke up this morning and saw an edge of frost framing the window and I thought of my father and I thought of the cabinet downstairs in the den and I lay there, barely breathing, and then

I got up and knew where I was going. But I stalled, I delayed. I didn't leave for two hours because I am a coward, really. I am afraid of a thousand things, a million. Like, is it possible to be claustrophobic and yet fear open spaces, too? I mean, elevators panic me. I stand in the upright coffin and my body oozes sweat and my heart pounds and this terrible feeling of suffocation threatens me and I wonder if the doors will ever open. But the next day, I was playing center field—I hate baseball but the school insists on one participating sport—anyway, I stood there with all that immensity of space around me in center field and I felt as though I'd be swept off the face of the planet, into space. I had to fight a desire to fling myself on the ground and cling to the earth. And then there are dogs. I sat there in the house, thinking of all the dogs that would attack me on the way to Rutterburg, Vermont, and I told myself, This is crazy, I'm not going. But at the same time, I knew I would go. I knew I would go the way you know a stone will drop to the ground if you release it from your hand.

I went to the cabinet in the den and took out the gift for my father. I wrapped it in aluminum foil and then wrapped it again with newspaper, Scotch-taping it all securely. Then I went down to the cellar and got the pants and shoes and jacket, but it took me at least a half hour to find the cap. But I found it: the cap I needed, my father's old cap. It would be cold on the road to Vermont and this cap is perfect, woolen, the kind that I could pull over my ears if the cold became a problem.

Then I raided my savings. I have plenty of money. I have thirty-five dollars and ninety-three cents. I have enough money to travel first class to Vermont, in the Greyhound bus that goes all the way to Montreal, but I know that I am going by bike to Rutterburg, Vermont. I don't want to be confined to a bus. I want the open road before me, I want to sail on the wind. The bike was waiting in the garage and that's how I wanted to go. By bike, by my own strength and power. For my father.

I looked at myself in the mirror before I left, the full-length mirror on the side of the closet door in my parent's bedroom upstairs. I inspected myself in the mirror, the crazy hat and the old jacket, and I knew that I looked ridiculous. But what the hell, as Amy says, philosophically.

I thought longingly of Amy. But she was at school and almost impossible to call. I could have faked it. I could have called the school and pretended that I was her father and asked to speak to her, saying that there was an emergency at home. Her father is editor of the Monument *Times* and always speaks with emergency in his voice, his sentences like headlines.

But I have to be in the mood to pull off a stunt like that—in fact, those kinds of stunts are Amy's specialty. And besides, my mind was on the road to Vermont. I love Amy Hertz. It's ridiculous that her name is Hertz—she's probably heard a thousand car-rental jokes and I have vowed never to make one. Anyway, I decided not to call her. Not until I'm away. I will call her on the way to Rutterburg, Vermont. And I will soothe myself by thinking of her and her Numbers and all the times she let me kiss her and hold her. But I didn't want to think about all that as I prepared for my journey.

I went to the kitchen and took out the bottle of pills from the cabinet and decided not to take one. I wanted to do this raw, without crutches, without aid, alone. I opened the bottle of pills and turned it over and let the pills fall out—they are capsules, actually, green and black—and I watched them disappear into the mouth of the garbage disposal. I felt strong and resolute.

I got the bike out of the garage and walked down the driveway, guiding the bike before I swung into the seat. I had my father's package in the basket above the front wheel. I was traveling light, with no provisions or extra clothing.

Finally, I leaped onto the bike, feeling reckless and courageous. At that moment, the sun came out, dazzling and brilliant: an omen of good fortune. I swung out into the street and a car howled its horn at me for straying too far into the roadway— and I wavered on the bicycle, the front wheel wobbling. I thought, This is ridiculous, this trip to Rutterburg. I almost turned back. But I didn't. I thought of my father and I started pedaling away, and I gained momentum and knew I would go, nothing would stop me, nothing.

And now I am leaving Monument and crossing the town line into Aswell. A sign by the side of the road says that the Aswell Rotary Club meets every Monday at noon. I have only gone four or five miles and my legs don't feel strong anymore. My legs are weary and my back sings with pain because I am out of condition. Frankly, I have never been in condition, which is a source of delight to Amy Hertz who dislikes all kinds of physical exercise.

I keep pedaling despite the weariness and the pain. I am determined to go to Rutterburg. I suck in the cold air and it caresses my lungs. My forehead is damp with sweat and I pull the cap down over my ears. I have all those miles to go.

"Take it easy," I tell myself. "Take it easy. One mile at a time."

And suddenly there's a long hill slanting down before me and the bike picks up speed and my legs are whirling madly, without effort, the bike carried by the momentum, and I let myself join the wind, soaring over the road as I coast beautifully down into Aswell.

T: Good morning. My name is Brint. We
       shall be spending some time together.
       (5-second interval.)

A: Good morning.

T: Shall we begin immediately? I have been
       advised that you are ready. The sooner
       we begin, the better it will be for you.

A: I'm not sure where to begin.

T: First, you must relax. And then let your
       thoughts flow. Take your time—there is no
       cause for hurry. Go back if you wish—
       back to your earliest remembrance.
       (8-second interval.)
A: It's hazy—just a series of impressions.
T: Let the impressions come.
       (5-second interval.)
A: That night—
T: Tell me about that night.
A: It's as if I was born that night. I mean,
       became a person, a human being in my own
       right. Before that, nothing. Or those
       impressions again—lights—smell—
       perfume, the perfume my mother always
       wore, lilac. Nothing else. And then that
       night—
       (12-second interval.)
T: Tell me about it.

He was in bed and the sheets were twisted around him and his body was hot, his eyes like raw onions, head aching. He cried out once or twice, softly, tentatively. He lifted his head toward the door. The door was partially open, allowing a slant of feeble light into the room. He curled up in bed, listening. He always liked to listen at night. Often he heard his mother and father murmuring in their bedroom, the bed making a lot of noise, and there were the nice sounds of his father and mother together, making soft sounds as if they were furry animals like the stuffed animals he always slept with, Bittie the Bear and Pokey the Pig, his friends. His father would say: "Hey, boy, you're getting too old for all those toys, three and a half, going on four." The boy knew that his father was joking, that he would never take his friends away. Anyway, his mother would say: "Now, now, he's a long time from four, a long long time." The tenderness in her voice and her perfume like lilac in the spring.

Now the boy cuddled in the bed with Pokey the Pig, his favorite, clutched to his chest. But something kept him awake, prevented him from sleeping. Out of the half-dark of the house, he realized that his mother's and father's voices were different, not soft and murmuring the way they usually were at night, but louder. Not really louder but harsher. They were speaking in whispers but their voices scratched at the night and the dark. And he heard his mother say, "Shh. You might wake him."

The boy lay still, as unmoving as Pokey the Pig.

The bed creaked in the next room, and he heard his father's bare feet padding toward his room. His figure blocked out the slant of light. Then his father's footsteps receded, the light spilled into the room again, and the boy felt brave and clever, knowing he had fooled his father. He wanted to tell Pokey how clever he was but he remained still and silent, not daring to move, listening not only with his ears but his entire being.

T: What did you hear?
A: I'm not sure. What I mean is, I don't

know whether I actually heard the words
or if I'm filling them in now, like blank
spaces on a piece of paper you have to
complete. I was barely three and a half,
I guess. Anyway, I knew they were
discussing me. More than that. As if they
were discussing what to do about me. And
I got all panicky and began to cry. But
quiet crying so they wouldn't hear me.
(*5-second interval.*)

T: Why this panic?

A: Well, it's as if they were deciding my fate.
I thought they were going to send me away.
I heard my mother say, "But what do we
tell him?" And my father saying, "It
doesn't matter, he's too young to realize
what's happening." Did I really hear him
saying that or did the sense of what he was
saying come to me? Then they began
talking about a trip, the three of us, and
I felt better. It was winter outside, snow
and cold, and I didn't want to leave the
house where it was nice and warm, but as
long as we were together, I really didn't
care.

T: Do you remember the trip?

A: Vaguely again. I remember a journey.
Endless. On a bus, the terrible smell of the
exhaust. The doors hissed like a snake
when they opened. Impressions. Crowded,
with luggage. Faces, my father's cigarettes,
not the smell of smoke, really, but the

smell of his matches, the sulphur of the
matches. Strange . . .
(6-second interval.)

T: What's strange?

A: I was always aware of two smells, my
      mother's perfume and the way my father
      always smelled of tobacco or smoke or the
      matches. But after that night, after the
      bus trip, I don't associate my father with
      cigarettes anymore. Because my father
      doesn't smoke. I've never seen him smoke
      a cigarette. But my mother's perfume was
      the same.

T: Do you remember anything else about
      the trip?

A: Not specifically. Mostly, the mood, the
      feeling of the trip, as if—

T: As if what?

A: It was spooky, scary but not in a haunted
      house sort of way. But as if we were being
      chased, as if we were running away. I
      remember my mother's face as she looked
      out the window. She looked so sad, purple
      half-moons under her eyes. So sad. And
      the bus speeding through the night . . .
      (15-second interval.)

T: Anything else?

A: We never went back. Not back to what I
      thought was home. We were in a different
      home. A different house. A different aura
      to the house. It was still winter and cold
      and we were together, my mother and

father and me, but everything was different.

T: What it appears to be is this: Your family
moved. From one part of the country to
another. But not too far. It was still
winter where you went and winter where
you came from. A lot of families move.
Men are transferred in their jobs. Your
father could have been transferred as well.

A: Maybe.

T: Why are you hesitating? You appear—
uncertain.

A: I am.

T: About what?

A: I don't know.

But he did know. He didn't want to confide the
knowledge to the doctor, however. The doctor was
a complete stranger and although he seemed sympa-
thetic and friendly, he wasn't entirely comfortable
with him. It should have been easy to tell him
everything, all his doubts, to get it all off his chest,
but he wasn't sure how to proceed. He wondered
if he should tell him about the clues.

T: What clues?

A: What do you mean, "clues"?

T: What you just said—you used the word
"clues."

He retreated into silence, stunned. Could the doctor read his mind? Impossible. Or maybe the medicine was doing funny things again. The medicine

was always playing tricks on him. And now it was making him believe he was only thinking when he was actually speaking aloud. He would have to be careful. He would have to watch himself, to listen for his voice. The panic shivered in his bones and a terrible tingling took possession of his body.

A: I'd like to go back now.
T: Of course.
A: I'm tired.
T: I understand. Don't press. There's plenty
      of time.
A: Thank you.
T: Everything's going to be all right.

END TAPE OZK001

"Aswell. Fairfield. Carver!"

The man calls out the names like the train announcer at North Station in Boston.

"Fleming—Hookset—Belton Falls!"

His voice is gravelly, as if his throat is full of stones, and his words leap over them: "Belton Falls is smack on the New Hampshire–Vermont line. Then the next stop—your last stop—right across the river is Rutterburg, Vermont."

He consults the map again.

"You're lucky, Skipper," he says. "You're going to touch three states—Massachusetts where you're standing right this minute and then New Hampshire and Vermont. But you're traveling at an angle and you only have to cover about seventy miles to do it."

Seventy miles doesn't seem far. Standing here in the gasoline station, anxious to be on my way, my legs itching to pedal that bike, seventy miles seems insignificant.

The old man looks up from the map. "How fast you figure you can go, Skipper?"

I want to get away but he's a nice old man, white hair and a face with so many red and blue veins that it resembles the road map in his hands. I had stopped at the service station to rest and ask for a map and to check the air in the tires. The old man, who seemed to be just hanging around, was eager to help, using a gauge to measure the air and then hunting up a map.

"I figure I can make ten miles an hour," I say.

"Lucky if you make five. Or even four," the old man says. "I don't think you're going to make it today, Skipper."

"My mother and father and me—we once stayed in a great motel in Belton Falls. If I can make it that far, I can stay there tonight."

The old man squints at the map again. It flutters in the breeze. "Well, maybe. But there's other motels before then." He starts to fold the map. "Where you from, Skipper?"

"Monument." It has turned cold now and the sun has disappeared behind the clouds.

"Let's see—this is Aswell. How long did it take you to make it here from Monument?"

I really want to be going. "About an hour."

He strokes his chin with the map. The map bulges in his hand. He has done a terrible job of folding it. "Well, from downtown Monument to this very spot is about five miles. But you had some good hills to coast down. Five miles an hour— probably the best time you'll do all day."

"Yes."

He turns away and looks up at the sky and then back at me again. "What do you want to go for, Skipper? It's a terrible world out there. Murders and assassinations. Nobody's safe on the streets. And you don't even know who to trust anymore. Do you know who the bad guys are?"

I want to be going. I don't want to listen.

"Of course you don't. Because you can't tell the good guys from the bad guys anymore. Nobody knows these days. Nobody. No privacy, either. Next time you use a phone, you listen. Listen close. You might hear a click. And if you do, then somebody's listening. Even if you don't hear a click, somebody might be listening anyway."

I kick at the tire of the bike.

"Don't trust anybody, Skipper. Ask for identification if a stranger comes near you. But you can't trust identifications, either. They can forge anything today—passports, licenses, you name it. So if you have to go, Skipper, be careful. Be careful."

He hands me the road map. "Keep it," he says. It's spotted with grease and not folded right but I tuck it into the basket, sliding it between the strap and my father's package.

"You're a sight for sore eyes, Skipper," he says. "That cap you got on. Haven't seen one of them for years. In the old days, we called them *tooks*. The wife used to make them for the kids, with cut-rate wool she picked up at the mill."

"It's my father's cap," I say. "He kept it all these years. I'm going to visit him—he's in a hospital in Rutterburg and I figure he'll get a kick out of seeing the cap."

"That your father's jacket, too?" he asks. "Looks like one of them army fatigue jackets. I had a boy in the service. World War Two, that was. He wore a jacket like that. Looked too big for him, like yours. He got killed at a place called Iwo Jima you probably never heard of."

The blue veins are bulging out on his face, all mixed up with the red ones. I want to leave. I am getting nervous. I feel bad about his son, but I don't want to talk to him anymore. I'm afraid that he'll start asking about my father. And my mother.

"I'm sorry about your son," I say.

He doesn't say anything but he wipes his hand across his face and sighs heavily as if he is suddenly very tired. "Well, have a good trip, Skipper," he says, stroking the front tire. "If I was forty years younger, I'd go along with you. The spirit's willing but the flesh is weak, like they say."

I leap on the bike. I head for the road.

"Thanks," I yell, looking back at him. "Thanks for the map and the air in the tires."

He stands there, looking sad, hands hanging at his sides.

"Be careful now," he calls, his voice cracked by the wind.

I wave and turn away, pedaling hard.

I have a destination to reach, and the old man is already in the past.

I am away. I am with the wind and the sun. I am the bike and the bike is me.

T: Now tell me, should we discuss Paul
      Delmonte?

A: Who?

T: Paul Delmonte.
      (8-second interval.)

A: I'd prefer not to.
      (5-second interval.)

T: Amy Hertz, then?

A: My headache is returning.

T: Relax for a moment. I shall send for medication.

A: I'd rather not have medication right now.

T: As you wish.
       (10-second interval.)

T: You seem upset. Please relax. Realize that the tension and the headache are anxiety reactions. And I'm sorry you are reacting this way. When we undertook these talks, we agreed that they must be voluntary on your part, that I would act merely as a guide. I would not take you to places where you do not wish to venture, into territory you do not wish to invade.

A: I understand.

T: We can return to Paul Delmonte and Amy Hertz another time.

A: My head really hurts. I feel nauseous, too.

T: Let us suspend then.

A: Thank you.

END TAPE OZK002

The road is long and level and straight, and there are no dogs in sight and the sun is shining. I sing as I pedal along:

> *The farmer in the dell,*
> *The farmer in the dell,*
> *Heigh-ho, the merry-o,*
> *The farmer in the dell.*

The cars speed past me because Route 119 is a state highway with a faded yellow line in the middle of it like an old ribbon left out in the rain too long. I sometimes steer the bike onto the sand of the soft shoulder, afraid that a car might hit me if I stray too far into the road itself. The wheels slide on the sand and I almost lose my balance. I keep singing:

> *The farmer takes a wife,*
> *The farmer takes a wife,*
> *Heigh-ho, the merry-o,*
> *The farmer takes a wife.*

I try to sing the song the way my father always sings it, comically, making his voice go up and down, then loud and soft. He has a terrible singing voice—"You have a tin ear," my mother always says—but he always gets a kick out of singing that particular song. "It's our song," he says. I can remember how he'd pick me up when I was just a kid and swing me almost to the ceiling, singing:

> *The wife takes the child,*
> *The wife takes the child . . .*

And then he'd gently place me in my mother's lap where she'd be sitting, knitting or reading, and I would curl into her body, feeling warm and safe and protected from all the bad things in the world. I was only five or six at the time, I guess. And my father sang raucously and joyously:

> *Heigh-ho, the merry-o,*
> *The farmer in the dell.*

"Dave, Dave," my mother would say. "You're a nut, a real nut." There was laughter and tenderness in her voice, and the lilac of her perfume surrounded me.

"Hey, what other family has a theme song tailor-made for them?" my father would say, acting the clown now, prancing around the room.

> *The child takes the cat,*
> *The child takes the cat . . .*

"They didn't make up the song for us," my mother would say, falling in with the old game that always delighted me. This was in the days before she became sad, of course.

"Who says they didn't make up the song for us?" my father would ask. Looking down at me, he'd say, "What's your name, boy?" Pretending to be very serious now.

"Adam," I'd answer. "Adam Farmer." Glad to be a part of the game, a part of them.

"Right," my father would say. "Suppose our name was Smith? Did you ever hear anybody singing 'Mr. Smith in the dell, Mr. Smith . . .'"

"Oh, David," my mother would say. And I'd laugh with delight and my father would begin singing again the way I sing now on Route 119:

> *Heigh-ho, the merry-o,*
> *The child takes the cat . . .*

The day is suddenly glorious, the October trees burning in the sun, colors rioting, hectic reds and browns. Sometimes the wind rises, startling a flock of birds into flight, sending leaves tumbling through the air and onto the highway. I pass a long meadow where cows lounge lazily, chewing their cuds.

I am glad that I didn't take the pills and I sing:

> *The cat takes the rat,*
> *The cat takes the rat,*
> *Heigh-ho, the merry-o,*
> *The cat takes the rat . . .*

I try to keep singing like my father but I have lost the touch. The wind catches at my throat and I realize I have to conserve my breath. My lungs burn and I figure I'd better stop singing for a while. My shoulders throb with pain and my fingers ache where they grip the handlebars.

A hill confronts me, sloping upward endlessly.

I look behind me: nothing.

I get off the bike and stare at the hill.

I start pushing the bike and walk along beside it. I don't like to walk that way because I feel vulnerable. And I have to go to the john now. I should have gone at that gas station back in Aswell. I could go into the woods but I hesitate to stray from the road. Who knows what lurks in the woods? I am not only afraid of dogs but all animals, plus snakes and spiders. They are not rational. So I need to stay on the road and keep moving, keep moving, even if I am tired. I reach the top of the hill and a beautiful vista is spread below me. A mile or so away, a cluster of buildings and a white church steeple stabbing the sky. And

I leap onto my bike again and start down the hill, down, down, seeking again my old friend momentum, and the bike gathers speed and I am sailing now, sailing sweetly, and I am dashing toward that church steeple, heading toward it so swiftly that it seems I could become impaled on it if I lose control of the bike. I am slanting down the hill and the wind eats at my cheeks, biting chunks out of my flesh, and I begin to sing again, trying to sound like my father and failing, but singing just the same:

> *The farmer in the dell,*
> *The farmer in the dell . . .*

The wind takes my voice and scatters it in the air and it disappears like smoke.

I hit the straightaway.

I am hurtling now, really zooming, and the trees and the telephones flash by.

> *Heigh-ho, the merry-o,*
> *The farmer in the dell . . .*

My voice breaks loud and clear against the wind, and I breeze on, feeling at last that I am really and truly on the way to Rutterburg, Vermont.

TAPE OZK003   0845   date deleted T-A

T: Shall we continue?
         (8-second interval.)
T: Do you feel well?
         (5-second interval.)
T: You seem unhappy, distracted. Is there
         anything wrong?
         (15-second interval.)

T :   Have you been administered your medicine
        today?
        (10-second interval.)

He had stepped outside himself, departed, gone
from this place and was outside looking in, watching himself and the doctor, if he was a doctor. He
could be a doctor, he had a kindly face although
sometimes his eyes were strange. The eyes stared
at him occasionally as if the doctor—if that's what
he was—were looking down the barrel of a gun,
taking aim at him. He felt like a target. That's
why he was glad that he could stand aside like this,
step out of himself and look back and see the two
of them there in the room. He was curious about
himself, of course, but he really didn't want to
look at himself and so he kept his eyes directed at
his questioner, obliterating himself from the view.
He hadn't realized he could be so clever, so cunning. And he thought, "If I can step outside myself
like this, maybe I can go to other places." The
possibility delighted him, made him forget. Forget
what? He wasn't sure—something—something just
hovering at the edge of his mind, scurrying away
when he tried to capture it . . .

T :   Perhaps we should postpone.
        (5-second interval.)
T :   There is no hurry. We shall try again
        later.

END TAPE OZK003

The dog is ferocious and I am terrified.

He is waiting for me at the end of a long flat stretch at the bottom of the hill. I had seen him waiting for a long distance when he was only a small, silent lump at the side of the road. Then, as I drew nearer, he revealed himself as a German shepherd, sleek and black, a silent sentinel guarding the driveway of a big white house. The house is set back from the road. I sense that the house

is deserted, that I am alone out here with the dog.
I pump furiously, wanting to sail by the dog as
fast as possible, so fast that I will dazzle him with
my speed and leave him stunned by my passing.

The dog lifts his head at my approach, alert,
ears sharp, as if he is accepting a challenge. My
eyes swing quickly, left to right and back again,
but there are no rescuers in sight. The driveway
behind the dog is empty, no cars in sight, and the
house itself wears an abandoned look, as if the
people have all gone away. Across the street, an
open field lies behind a wandering low stone wall.

As I approach, the dog steps out into the road
and I think, It's as if he has been waiting for me
all my life. The dog is unmoving, his tail not
wagging, his eyes like marbles. He is silent, watchful, a killer dog. I am close enough now to see
how his sleek hair is shiny, and I tell myself, Let's
go, it's just a dog, a dog is man's best friend, it's
not a lion or a tiger.

The dog makes a move, steps into the roadway
directly in the path of the bike, his head lifted
now, a snarl on his lips. He is silent, he has not
barked or growled or maybe I can't hear the growl
as the wind rushes past my ears. I pedal hard,
crouched on the bike, fingers clutching the handlebars, legs pumping away, the bike aimed directly
for him, afraid that if I try to steer around him,
I will somehow lose my balance and be flung to the
pavement, at his mercy on the pavement. I slit my
eyes and my legs slash away and I hurtle toward
the dog. And at the last possible moment the dog

darts aside, and now I hear his growl and then the growl erupts into short sharp savage barks and this is worst of all because the barks reveal his teeth.

The dog keeps trying to dash in front of the bike, as if he is more interested in stopping the bike than in attacking me. I take heart at this. The dog bites at the front tire and turns away as the tire scrapes his nose and the wheel wobbles frantically. And I keep yelling to myself, *It's all right, it's all right,* but my words are lost on the wind and inside I am saying, The hell with this, if I get away from this dog, I'm going home, I'm taking the first bus back, the hell with Rutterburg, Vermont, the hell with everything . . .

The bike is in danger of toppling now as the dog continues to attack the front wheel and I realize with horror that this has been its intention from the beginning: to topple the bike, send it askew and have me crashing to the roadway, his victim.

We are past the driveway now and approaching a curve. I hope desperately that there is safety around the curve, a house or a store or a shack or anything. That's when I hear a car approaching and a horn frantically blowing. I suddenly realize that I have drifted perilously close to the center of the road. The oncoming car, a yellow Volkswagen with luggage lashed to the roof, has to cut speed and swerve to avoid hitting me, the blast of the horn joined by the squeal of brakes. The dog is distracted by the car and the honking and the screeching and it hesitates for a moment, pausing almost in mid-air, looking at the car as if puzzled. Or tempted. I keep pedaling. But I can't resist looking behind me and I see the dog streaking away, down the road in pursuit of the VW, barking wildly, body arched and stretched, a fuzzy furry arrow.

"Let's get out of here," I yell to nobody and renew my pedaling, fear and panic having obliterated any weariness, any aching muscles. The barking of the dog grows distant as I swoop around the curve and sail steadily onward.

I am approaching the main street of Fairfield and it is hardly a Main Street and hardly a town, just a few stores and that church with the white steeple and I speed through the street, carried by my momentum. I know I should stop but I don't want to get off the bike. I want to keep going, to get to Rutterburg. I have a feeling that the dog will pursue me forever, will wait for me outside stores if I stop to eat or go to the john. I open my mouth and gulp air and the rush of air is sweet in my lungs and I feel strong again as the air caresses my lungs. I pedal through the town, across a wooden bridge, the sound of the slats like applause in my ears. And I say hello and goodbye to Fairfield and continue on my way, feeling as though I will never stop, never stop.

TAPE OZK004   0800   date deleted T-A

A: Are you a doctor?
T: Why do you ask?
A: Well, I've taken it for granted that you are
       a doctor, a psychiatrist maybe. That first
       session—you said your name is Brint.
       But you didn't say "Doctor Brint." And
       this place seems to be a hospital. But is it?

T: I am happy to see you taking an interest in your surroundings. For a long time, you did not do so. But what makes you think this place may or may not be a hospital?

A: Well, it doesn't smell like one. You know— hospitals have a medicine smell. And high white beds. The doctors wear white coats, the nurses dress in white, too. But not here. This place is more like—

T: Like what?

A: I don't know. A private home. Not merely a home but an estate. All the rooms and all these people. A private sanitorium maybe.

T: Does this bother you?

A: I don't know. There are so many things I don't know.

T: Then, let's find them out, shall we? (*5-second interval.*)

T: Those clues, for instance.

A: What clues?

T: You mentioned something about clues earlier.

He was wary again, on guard, distrustful. Yet he had no reason to distrust Brint, even though he was a stranger. Anyway, he was feeling much better, and he didn't even care if feeling better was only an illusion. Maybe he should tell Brint some of the clues. Not all, but some. He could do it because he felt good, in command. He could parcel out information as if he were dealing cards, a little at a time. But he would have to be clever, cunning.

A: Maybe the dog is a clue.
T: The dog?
A: Yes, the dog. I thought of the dog when I looked out this morning and saw a dog on the grass.
T: You mean Silver?
A: Is that his name? Silver? A German shepherd?
T: Yes, a good dog.
A: I hate dogs.
T: All dogs?
A: Most of them.
T: Why is that?
         (10-second interval.)
T: You said the dog is a clue. You mean Silver? Or some other dog?
A: Some other dog.
T: Tell me.

The dog wasn't big but it made up for its lack of size by its ugliness, the intensity of its eyes and the way it stood there, implacable, blocking their path. There was something threatening about the dog, a sense that the rules didn't apply, like encountering a crazy person and realizing that anything could happen, anything was possible.

"What kind of dog is that?" the boy asked, whispering.

"I don't know, Adam," his father said. "I don't know much about dogs."

"What do we do, Dad?"

"We bluff."

The boy looked up at his father in wonder and disbelief. Suddenly, this man did not seem like his father. His father was an insurance agent who went to the office every day and changed his car every two years and belonged to the Rotary Club. He wore horn-rimmed glasses and had a mustache —not a shaggy mustache like the ones people wore who also had long hair but a neat trimmed mustache with glints of gray. Adam had always been aware of his father as a *father,* reading the newspaper, watching baseball and football on television, rooting for the Red Sox and cursing the Patriots, bringing work home from the office at night, reading the newspaper, kissing him good night with a peck on the forehead. A father. Like a cutout figure whose caption said *Father.* The only time his father emerged as a person was when the subject of books came up. His father's eyes would shine and he'd shake his head with wonder as he discussed this writer or that writer—writers like Hemingway and Fitzgerald and a lot of others who stirred no recognition in Adam when he was a child. "Wait until you get older, Adam, there are so many great books to be read." His father often could be found reading late into the night, slumped in his chair, the glasses perched on his long thin nose, lost in the pages of a book, a sudden stranger in the house.

Now his father seemed like a stranger again, as they stood in the woods confronting the dog. He and his father weren't the kind of people who ordinarily strolled through the woods. City pavement was more natural under their shoes than grass or woodland paths. "Give me Mother Nature working nervously in neon," his father once said, "instead of turning the leaves all kinds of colors in the fall." Then what were they doing here in the first place, in the woods, at least a mile from nowhere? Adam wasn't sure. Actually, they had been heading for the library, a mid-afternoon stroll on a wind-tossed March Saturday. Adam loved to walk along with his father, trying to match his nine-year-old stride to his father's loping legs. They'd walk along and his father would have to slow down once in a while so that he wouldn't get too far ahead. His father loved the library—a treasure house, he called it. All those books, all those records. Today, he said, they'd look for Louis Armstrong records and bring them home. Great stuff that Adam also would love—a marvelous old record called "Twelfth Street Rag" in which Louis Armstrong made his trumpet sound like a man staggering drunk along the street. Ah, that Armstrong. His father could do that—arouse Adam's interest by making him curious: How could a trumpet possibly sound like a man staggering along a street? Or, he'd say, "I'll show you a mystery novel in which the first two letters of the first word of the first chapter hold the secret to the book!" ("When, Dad, when?")

Anyway, they were on their way to the library for the Armstrong record, bending against the dancing wind, when suddenly his father stopped in his tracks, and Adam, who had been holding his hand, was thrown off balance and almost fell. He looked up at his father, puzzled. His father stood there like a statue in the park, or as if stricken by some terrible disease that had paralyzed him.

"Let's go," his father said, finally snapping into action. He tugged at Adam's arm. He almost dragged him around the corner and through a narrow alley between Baker's Drugstore and Admadio's Furniture.

"Hey, Dad," Adam cried. "Where are we going? The library's not this way."

"I know, I know," his father said, plunging into one of his imitations, this time W. C. Fields, an old-time movie comedian who talked out of the side of his mouth, giving forth fancy and ridiculous words as his father was now doing. "Let us stalk other landscapes as we ponder the wonders of the third month of the year, my boy." His voice nasal and his fingers flicking the ash from an invisible cigar as he hurried along, pulling Adam with him.

Adam looked behind—they seemed to be running away. But from who? From what?

"Ah, the woods," his father said, still W. C. Fields as he indicated the beginning of a section of trees and brush that ran for a mile or so toward the state highway.

As they entered the wooded area, he saw his

father glance backward. Adam followed the glance
—still nobody there.

"Everything all right, Dad?" he asked, lips trembling.

"Just fine, Adam, just fine," his father said in his
own voice.

So they plunged into the woods, tripping sometimes over tree limbs knocked down during winter
storms, crashing through brush as if they were on
safari in Africa, and after a while Adam began to
enjoy himself.

"Hey, Dad, this is kind of fun," Adam said.

His father, breathing hard, tousled Adam's hair.
"Not as bad as I thought it would be," he said.

Adam felt a sense of camaraderie. And that was
when they encountered the dog, like an apparition
from nowhere, ugly, unidentifiable, a piglike snout,
glittering eyes, and yellowed teeth.

"This is ridiculous," his father said now.

Adam knew what his father meant by ridiculous.
Here they were being frightened and intimidated
and held at bay by, of all things, a dog. Not an
armed robber. Not a wild animal. But a dog. Adam
felt, in fact, that he and his father might have been
running away from a greater danger behind them.
But that danger evaporated in the presence of the
dog. The dog looked capable of attack and violence,
the low growl in its throat menacing, deadly.

"Let's back up a little," his father said.

But the movement brought a loud growl from
the animal. The boy's heart began to beat wildly.

"Look, Adam. We've got to do something about this."

"But what, Dad?" Adam asked, feeling his chin trembling.

"First, I want you to get out of here."

"I want to stay with you, Dad."

"Look, the dog will probably let one of us go. Here's what to do. I'll take a small step forward— you take a big one backward. That might confuse him. Then take another one while I make a slight movement. But go slow. Don't upset the beast. Just walk backward. Keep going . . ."

"Where will I go?"

"I heard traffic a while ago. The highway runs to our left." His father was talking softly, barely moving his lips. "Make it to the highway and flag down a car."

"But what about you, Dad?"

"I think I can handle it alone. I'll try moving back," he said.

"I want to stay with you, Dad." Actually he wanted to get away, he was terrified of the dog, but he felt as though he'd be betraying his father if he left.

"You'll be helping most by going, Adam," his father said, finality in his voice. "Now, do it slowly . . ."

Adam retreated reluctantly, backing up slowly, not daring to glance at the dog, keeping his eyes on the ground, hoping he wouldn't trip and find himself on the ground, the dog rushing at him. He heard his father muttering, "A dog, for crissakes." The dog didn't move. Adam glanced up, the dog's ferocious eyes were on his father.

Adam took one more step—and the dog attacked, the growl reaching a siren's howl as the animal leaped toward his father. His father stepped aside, one arm outstretched, the dog's teeth ripping the sleeve of his father's jacket. The teeth caught on the jacket for a moment, long enough for his father to fling the animal away, changing its course for an instant. In that instant, his father cried for Adam to run, but Adam was frozen with horror to the spot. His father crouched low, close to the ground, meeting the dog at its level. But Adam saw that his father's right hand was searching the ground for a weapon, a stone or a stick. The dog, too, was crouched, body sloped forward, chin almost touching the ground. Adam's father slowly rose from the crouched position; he held a tree limb in his hand. The limb was about an inch thick. He thrust it toward the dog, as if offering the animal a gift. For the first time, the animal seemed confused, the glittering eyes wavering in their intensity. Then without warning, the dog leaped again—but this time at the limb, grasping it with its teeth. His father grabbed the limb with both hands and swung it as the dog closed its jaws around it. He swung furiously, the dog hanging on frantically. Suddenly his father let go of the limb, allowed it to soar away from him, the dog still gripping it in its teeth. Thrown off balance and spinning dizzily in the air, the dog fell awkwardly to the ground, howling now, scurrying to its feet. Adam's father grabbed another branch, and another. He held tree limbs in each hand now. He looked like a lion tamer in a movie.

"Come on, you bastard," his father yelled at the dog.

Adam had never heard his father swear like that before, although he said "hell" and "damn" once in a while. The sound coming from the dog was not a growl anymore but a kind of cry, a moan, as if it had been injured. And then, as suddenly as it had appeared, it departed, pawing the ground one moment and then turning away the next, thrashing through bushes and thicket.

Adam's father turned, mouth open, breath coming in huge gasps, his cheek streaked with dirt and sweat, jacket torn. Adam rushed to him, flung his arms around him. He had never loved his father as much as at that moment.

T: And that was the clue?

A: I think so. You said to tell it all from the beginning, if possible. And this was the beginning.

T: What strikes you as important about that incident?

A: What do you mean?

T: I mean—was the encounter with the dog in the woods most important? Or was it what made you and your father enter the woods? (*5-second interval.*)

A: At the time, my father and I didn't talk

about why we went into the woods. We didn't say anything to my mother—it was as if we shared a secret. And the dog was such a terrifying experience that it overshadowed everything else. I hadn't seen anyone following us. My father told my mother that he had felt like taking a walk in the woods because it was the first nice day in March. And by the time it was all over— they found the dog had actually bitten my father and he needed a shot at the hospital— I'd forgotten about the reason why we went into the woods.

T: What do you think your father saw on the street that made him panic?

A: I don't know. Even now, I'm not sure he did panic. I'm telling it the way I remembered but that was a long time ago. I was only nine.

T: But you felt at the time that your father was in flight through the woods?

A: Yes.

T: What do you suppose he saw?

A: I don't know. I don't know.
(*5-second interval.*)

A: May we take a break? I'm tired—drained.

T: Of course. You did well. Try to rest now.

A: Thank you.

END TAPE OZK004

The telephone booth stands outside Howard Johnson's at the junction of Routes 99 and 119, and the
sun splashes on the windows and glass doors of the
booth. I get off my bike and walk toward the booth.
My shoe rubs against a blister on the heel of my
right foot. I bend against the wind and start to
search for change in my pocket. I need to talk to
Amy Hertz; her voice will sustain me. I should
have called her this morning before I left Monu-

ment. I should have taken the medicine. I should have stopped in Fairfield and gone to the john or at least bought something to eat, even if only a Hershey bar. Now I am somewhere between Fairfield and Carver and there are all those other places ahead to go through and I am discouraged. I get discouraged very easily. That's why I need to talk to Amy. She refreshes my spirit, she makes me laugh. I love her.

I reach the telephone booth after an endless walk, like in a dream when you can't reach your destination, and I look at my watch and find out that it's only 1:15. School doesn't end until 2:15, and it takes her at least fifteen minutes to get home if she doesn't stop on the way. I look at the telephone in the booth with disgust. Not disgust for the phone but disgust at myself. I have lost all track of time. I will never reach Belton Falls by darkness at this rate and I have to go to the john. I glance at Howard Johnson's. I'm not hungry but I know that my body requires food for energy, fuel for my trip to Rutterburg. My mother always says that I don't eat enough and she is always trying to get food into me or bringing home the latest vitamin discovery in the form of candy or chewing gum. My poor mother. I walk my bike to the door of Howard Johnson's. When I was just a little kid, I called it "Orange Johnson" and we were driving along in the car, my mother and father and me, I was between them in the front seat, and when I said "Orange Johnson" the first time they laughed and laughed and I felt safe and secure and surrounded by love. And sometimes in the night even now I murmur "Orange Johnson" in the dark and feel good again, safe again.

I really have to go to the john now. I know Howard Johnson's has rest rooms, but there are at least two problems. First of all, what can I do with the bike? There is no lock and I can't risk leaving it unguarded because somebody might steal it and I would be marooned here if that happened. The second problem is this: Suppose the bathroom in Howard Johnson's has no window? That will create all kinds of complications because I can't stand places without windows. Then I see an immediate solution to the bike problem. The booths are located near the windows and I will sit in a booth, close to the door, and be able to keep an eye on the bike. The second problem is also quickly solved, and I figure that my luck is turning. From my vantage point, I can see a Sunoco station across the street and the rest room sign is visible and there is a window in the door of the one that says *Men*. Now that relief is imminent, I really have to go to the john and I hurry across the street.

Later, I stand in the telephone booth and the telephone rings and rings. I know it's a long shot, I know that Amy Hertz is still in school, but I figure that maybe she came home early. But the phone keeps on ringing and I lose count of the rings.

My stomach is tight and tense. The hamburger I ate in Howard Johnson's has turned into a rock in my stomach. I should have ordered something easy to digest: soup or chowder. And I should have taken the medicine with me. My hand is glued with perspiration to the receiver and my fingers feel strange and alien—they are accustomed to the contours of the bike's handlebars. A headache has begun: iron bars beneath the flesh of my forehead. I am a wreck, but Amy Hertz, even the voice of Amy Hertz, could cure all that.

The phone is still ringing, unendingly.

The trucks are headed north on Interstate 99 and their motors grind and groan, lonesome sounds.

The operator cuts in. "I'm sorry. Your party does not answer."

The operator is a man and it's startling to hear a man's voice on the line.

"Will you try a few more times?" I ask, although I know it is futile. Yet, somehow, I find it comforting to know that the phone is ringing in Amy's home, echoing in the rooms where she eats and sleeps and reads her books and watches television.

After a while, the operator says, "I'm sorry, sir. There is still no answer."

"Thank you," I say. "Thank you for trying."

Immediately, the coins come tumbling out of the phone and I slip them out of the coin-return slot. I push open the door of the booth—it sticks for a minute and my heart pounds: Will I be trapped inside?—but it finally opens again and I step outside. The sun has disappeared and the clouds are low, pressing downward, almost claustrophobic. Rutterburg seems far away, impossible to reach. My stomach lurches with nausea and my head throbs. I walk toward the bike and my blister hurts. If I could have talked with Amy . . .

My next stop is Carver and I check my map. The mileage chart says that one inch represents ten miles and Carver is only about one-half inch away. By the time I reach Carver, Amy should be home from school. And maybe I can find a drugstore in Carver and buy aspirins for my headache. I check the bike and I lash my father's present to the basket. I pull the cap down over my ears—it keeps me warm and shuts out the lonesome sounds of the trucks laboring up the hill on Interstate 99. I looked behind but nobody is following me. In Carver, I can probably find a restaurant and order some soup or chowder.

I get on the bike and tell my legs, Pedal, pedal. It's as if I have been pedaling forever. I sing to keep up my spirits:

> *The farmer in the dell,*
> *The farmer in the dell . . .*

But I only sing for a little while because I am tired and I just want to hold on until I reach Carver.

TAPE OZK005   1350   date deleted T-A

T: Shall we discuss Amy Hertz?
A: If you want to.
       (5-second interval.)
T: Would you describe her as your best
       friend? Or more?

More. He thought of the night he and Amy had
huddled together under the football stands, the

field deserted, winter winds blowing, and how their lips had touched and opened, her tongue darting swiftly seeking his and then touching, and he shivered, not with the cold, but with delight. He had felt her breasts against his chest and his breath came rapidly, his heart beating dangerously. God, how he loved her.

A: More than a friend.
T: Tell me about her.

Amy. Amy Hertz. Who loved mischief and was always on the prowl for mischief. Amy said that everybody took life too seriously. When he first met her, she said, "Know what's the matter with you, Ace? You don't laugh enough. You have this long look on your face. But there's hope, Ace, there's hope. I see the possibility of laughter in your baby blues."

She talked like that. Wise-guy talk but she had her serious moments. She could isolate herself with books for hours at a time. That's how they met: the books. She was going into the Monument Public Library and he was coming out and they collided at the door. The books they held in their arms spilled all over the place.

As they bent to retrieve them, Amy said, "Know what this reminds me of? This reminds me of those old Hollywood comedies you see on TV where the hero and the heroine meet ridiculously. I mean, you can picture the writers sitting around the studio saying, 'Well, how do they meet this time?'

And somebody says, 'I've got it. How about: she's going *into* the library with all these books and he's coming *out* with all these books . . .' "

They were on their knees at the library's entrance with people coming and going, stepping around them, and she was talking a mile a minute and he was wondering, Who was this crazy girl, anyway? By the time they had gathered their books —"Don't mix up yours with mine," she said, "it'll cost you a mint because mine are all a month overdue at least"—anyway, by the time they stood facing each other, out of breath somehow, he was madly in love with her. She told him that her name was Amy Hertz ("No car-rental jokes, please"). She was short and robust and freckled, and one of her front teeth was crooked, but her eyes were beautiful, blue, like the blue of his mother's best china. She also had wonderful breasts—she told him later that her breasts were an embarrassment to her, too large ("Try lugging these things all over town every day"), but he was in love with her even before he noticed them. He also loved her because she didn't laugh when he told her that someday he was going to be a famous writer like Thomas Wolfe. And he loved her even more when she didn't ask who Thomas Wolfe was. Or didn't confuse him with the hip writer Tom Wolfe. Later, of course, she confessed that she hadn't the slightest idea who Thomas Wolfe was.

"You look like a great candidate for the Number," Amy said that first day, appraising him through squinted eyes. She was farsighted but hated wearing glasses. "Shy maybe, but I think you're the type who doesn't lose his cool. And cool is needed for the Number."

"What's the Number?" he asked, bewildered and delighted at the same time, having never met anyone like Amy Hertz before.

"You'll find out, Ace. Tomorrow—after school. Meet me at the front door. If you're available, that is."

He literally spun out of the library, books clutched in his arms, taking a moment to watch through the window as Amy Hertz proceeded to the circulation desk to return her books. He felt exuberant, wanting to burst into song, his usual shyness gone. He wanted to speak to complete strangers and tell them what a marvelous day this was, how beautiful the sunshine was as it poured forth on Main Street, dazzling in its brightness, turning the world golden.

The next day he was waiting for her when she emerged from the school. "Glad to see you, Ace," she said, and he was swept along in her wake as she prattled on about school and classes and a terrible test in algebra that she was certain she had failed.

She stopped abruptly and turned toward him. "You're a shy one, aren't you? And you don't say much. Or is it because I haven't given you a chance?" Her eyes were blue flowers.

"I'm shy," he said, marveling how he really didn't feel shy in her presence. Ordinarily, he shunned strangers. His marks often suffered in school because, although he did well in written

tests and compositions, he was terrible in oral reci-
tations, speeches, anything that required the spot-
light of attention to be focused on him.

"How come I've never seen you around?" she
asked as they walked along.

He shrugged. "I don't know." But he did know,
of course. He was seldom "around." He usually
went straight home after school. His mother was
home, waiting for him, withdrawn in her room,
upset if he arrived a few minutes late, tense and
nervous if she didn't always know his whereabouts.
He sometimes wondered what had happened to
transform his mother from the laughing, tender
woman to whom the scent of lilac clung into the
pale and subdued and antiseptic woman who seldom left the house, who lurked behind window
curtains. Adam could feel her eyes following him
when he left the house. But he didn't want to tell
Amy Hertz about his mother; he'd feel like a trai-
tor to her. Anyway, his terrible shyness, his inabil-
ity to feel at ease with people, had nothing to do
with his mother. He felt it was his basic character;
he preferred reading a book or listening to old jazz
records in his bedroom than going to dances or
hanging around downtown with the other kids.
Even in the fourth or fifth grade, he had stayed on
the outskirts of the schoolyard watching the other
kids playing the games—Kick the Can was a big
thing in the fourth grade—anyway, he had never
felt left out: it was his choice. To be a witness, to
observe, to let the events be recorded within himself on some personal film in some secret compart-

ment no one knew about, except him. It was only later, in the eighth grade, when he knew irrevocably that he wanted to be a writer, that he realized he had stored up all his observations, all his emotions, for that purpose. How could he possibly tell Amy Hertz all this without sounding like some kind of a nut? Yet, the funny thing, the strange thing, was that he wanted to tell her.

They arrived at Amy's house and he waited while she changed into jeans. Amy's mother, a tall, thin woman, acknowledged her introduction to Adam without really looking at him—she was on the telephone making arrangements for a committee meeting of some sort—and then she dashed out of the house on the way to another committee meeting. Adam wondered whether he should call his mother. He had told her he'd be late today, detained at a meeting of the Literary Club, but he was a terrible liar and guilt assailed him now. He wondered whether he had made a mistake, meeting Amy Hertz after school like this. What did a girl like her want with someone like him? She was lightning, he was cloud. Gray cloud. He sensed a poem lurking in the words and wanted to scribble them down.

"I'll be right out," Amy called, distracting him. He decided not to call his mother. Amy was in the bathroom and Adam wandered in that direction, summoned by her voice. He could hear all the noises she made in there and he tried not to listen, his cheeks warm. He heard the sound of a toilet flushing and the water faucet running. Amy stepped out and saw the blood staining his cheeks. Amused, she said, "Look, Ace, don't let a few farts bother you. It's all part of nature and being alive." Later she told him that she had chosen the words deliberately. "A bit of shock therapy," she explained.

They made their way to the A&P and the Number. The basic idea of the Number was simple: to fill a shopping cart with as many items as possible and then abandon it somewhere in the store and leave the store without being detected. Amy, however, had gone far beyond this basic premise. She had concocted all kinds of variations. First of all, the conditions were different at various times of the week. For instance, a Tuesday afternoon was a serious challenge because there were few shoppers around and it was easy for store personnel to spot any suspicious actions. Thursday nights and Saturdays were busy times, but Amy also increased the risks. She'd insist that only canned goods could be loaded into the cart, or another time, only jars, and she'd rule out gallon jugs. Once she loaded an entire shopping cart with baby food; it must have contained five hundred jars. She abandoned it in front of the Kotex display.

God, but Amy Hertz was beautiful to watch when she was doing a Number. The process had to be carried out seriously, with no hint of mischief. Sometimes she'd carry a shopping list, a *real* list that they'd jot down at her house after school. She'd consult the list frequently as they shopped, frowning over brand names, muttering about prices. One time, she and Adam took along a little kid, a neighbor of hers, to give the Number a family countenance. Amy said the important thing was to act natural, as if they belonged there, and always to act a little angry, a little impatient, because that always intimidated people. Sometimes she even asked a clerk for assistance. "Hey, where are the sardines, anyway?" she'd demand, annoyed at the store for hiding the sardines somewhere. That Amy.

Amy was at her best on those busy Thursday nights. She would attempt to fill as many shopping carts as possible. "Listen," she told Adam, "with your help we can break all existing records." They proceeded to do just that. They established the record one Thursday night during a big anniversary sale. Working individually, they filled twelve carts—eight for Amy and four for Adam. The carts were piled dangerously high, and Amy topped each of them with a bunch of celery, like some grotesque centerpiece. They had abandoned the carts all over the store and were delighted when a clerk went by, glanced at a cart, looked puzzled, and then continued on his way. But Amy wasn't content to end it all so casually. She insisted that all the carts be brought together in the last aisle where the fruits and vegetables were displayed. They lined them up like soldiers at attention. "Don't rush, act nonchalant," Amy cautioned. She pronounced "nonchalant" the French way, without sounding the t.

Later they sat on the fender of a parked car in front of the store. From their vantage point, they could see the row of shopping carts. Every now and then, a shopper would notice the carts and stare curiously for a while, as if looking for a sign to explain their presence. One woman lifted a bunch of celery from one cart and placed it in hers. After a while, there was a flurry of activity from the clerks. Two of them had discovered the carts and stood there, hands on their hips, puzzled. Within a few minutes, five or six other clerks were looking at the carts, puzzled, mystified, scratching their heads, looking around suspiciously. The manager finally arrived, a small bald harassed-looking man. He exploded with fury. He waved his arms. He jumped up and down like a figure in a cartoon. The sheepish clerks began to move the carts away. All of it delighted Amy—her laughter was marvelous to hear.

"We did it, Ace." she said. "We did it."

That night, when he took her home, he kissed her for the first time. She was the first girl he had ever kissed and he swelled with a love and desire that caused his body to tremble.

T: Is Amy Hertz one of the clues?
A: I think so. But I wanted to keep her
       separate, separate from everything else.
       Especially after she phoned me that
       afternoon—
T: Phoned you?
A: Yes. I had told her when we first met that I
       had lived in Monument since I was four

years old. That my family had moved to
New England from a small town in
Pennsylvania. Rawlings, Pennsylvania.
Then one day . . .

Amy's voice was vibrant on the telephone.
"Are you busy, Ace?"
"No, what's going on?" A call from Amy was
always exciting. Sometimes she had an idea for a
new Number. Like going to the Holiday Inn early
in the morning and ghosting through the corridors
removing the *Do Not Disturb* signs from the door-
knobs or turning them to the side that said, in three
different languages, *Please Make Up Our Room
Early*. Sometimes she only wanted to talk. She'd
tell him the entire plot of a movie she'd just seen
on television. Other times, she'd say, "Talk to me.
Read me poetry." His voice quivering, he would
read her a poem he had written, pretending it was
the work of an obscure poet: "My love for you is
like a searching wind . . ."
But this call was different. "Look, Ace," she
said, "I'm at the newspaper. I dropped in to see my
father and he has a visitor. An editor from Rawlings, Pennsylvania, who was passing through and
decided to drop in for a visit. Isn't Rawlings where
you're from?"
Once again, Adam was swept with a series of
vivid impressions, the bus ride at night, the sense
of hurry.
Amy went on. "Listen, this guy says he's lived in

Rawlings all his life and he can't remember any Farmers there. Not *farmer* farmers, but your kind of Farmer. He says he's always known everybody in town. Didn't you say your father sold insurance in Rawlings?"

"I don't know," Adam said. "Why is it important?"

"Well, it's not important, really. This man's just visiting and when my father told him your family was also from Rawlings he thought he'd drop in and see your folks. Kind of like a reunion. Then he couldn't remember any Farmers ever being in Rawlings, not in the insurance business, and I figured I'd call to check. I thought you'd be curious about your old home town."

"I am curious," Adam said. But he was more puzzled than curious. He tried to sound cool—he didn't want Amy to hear the puzzlement in his voice.

"Well, how about your mother? What was her maiden name? Maybe he remembers your mother." Amy giggled. "Some men are like that."

"My mother's name was Holden. Louise Holden."

"Hold on. I'll see if it strikes sparks."

He heard muffled conversation as Amy apparently reported her findings to the visiting editor.

"Nope," Amy said, returning to the phone. "That doesn't ring a bell either. Hey, how long did you live there, anyway? Didn't you say you were born there?"

Adam was about to say: "I *was* born there. And

my parents were, too." But something made him remain silent. The memory of flight . . .

"You still there, Ace?"

"Look, Amy, I said we came to Monument from Rawlings—but I didn't say I was born there. You must have misunderstood. We lived there, oh, only a few months, I guess. And my father wasn't working during that time. He'd had an accident, hurt his leg. We came to Monument when we heard that there was an insurance agency for sale."

Adam was amazed at his ability to lie, the way his mind had been quick to invent a new set of circumstances for himself and his parents. But he wondered *why*? Why is it necessary to lie?

"Well, I figured it was something like that, Ace. Anyway, too bad—if Rawlings had been your old home town, your father and mother might have enjoyed meeting him. They could have had a reunion and all."

"Well, thanks anyway, Amy. I appreciate it."

T: Was that all?
A: Yes.
T: Did Amy ever mention that conversation again?
A: No. Never.
T: What did you think of the conversation and her questions?
A: I felt funny—strange.
     (*5-second interval.*)
A: Then I rationalized. I told myself that the editor from Rawlings had been mistaken.

He probably had a bad memory. And I
guess I tried not to think about it.
(*10-second interval.*)

T:　Then we have arrived at the second
landmark, haven't we?

A:　Have we?

T:　Permit me to summarize. The first
landmark was that day in the woods with
the dog. The important thing was what
drove you and your father into the woods.
The second landmark was that call from
Amy. You were nine years old at the first
landmark and fourteen at the second.

A:　I'm tired.

T:　It's early. Take your time. We are doing
so well.

A:　I don't want to talk anymore.

T:　You are thinking of Amy.

A:　Yes.

T:　Is it beginning to come back to you, all of it,
not only Amy?

A:　I don't know.

T:　Let it come. Remember, I'm here to help
you. But let it come. The medicine will help
and I will help. But—

A:　But it's up to me, isn't it? Whether I win or
whether I lose?

T:　Think about winning.

A:　But if I lose?

T:　Don't think about that. Don't think about
that.

A: Would losing be that terrible?
  (5-second interval.)
T: Let us suspend for now.
A: Thank you.

END TAPE OZK005

The rain begins without warning, slashing at my face, pelting my body. Clouds had gathered as I pedaled along toward Carver but they hadn't concerned me because the sun and the clouds had played disappearing games since my departure this morning. Then a sudden torrent greets me as I pump along a narrow section of Route 119. Mud kicks at my legs because the front tire has no fender, nothing to prevent the mud from splashing. The rain slants toward me and the bicycle. I am driving into the storm.

I draw up at the side of the highway and ponder the situation. Squinting, I see a house about a quarter of a mile away, but I don't want to get mixed up with people. Trees offer the only shelter and I push the bike toward a large maple, heavy with branches. The rain showers leaves down as I approach and I realize the tree won't offer much protection because most of the leaves have already fallen. I lean against the tree trunk in disgust. The rain is really coming down now, in wavering sheets, tossed by the wind. The cold enters my clothes, seeps into my skin and into my bones. My father's package is soaked and the road map is ruined. I pull my father's package off the bike and hug it to me, slipping it inside the jacket. The package is wet but I don't mind. The rain continues. I watch the map dissolving. And I am suddenly hungry, ravenous. I am starved. I can't ever remember being as hungry as this.

A car passes, a station wagon with wooden panels, and the driver looks back as if he might stop. But he doesn't. I wish he had stopped. I could have thrown the bike into the back of the car and have driven along warm and dry inside. But I'm also glad that he didn't stop.

"You are a nut," I tell myself, my voice sounding strange in my ears. The rain dances on the ground, the way water jumps and leaps if you drop it on a hot stove. I shrivel into myself, hugging myself, cold and damp and miserable. I am not damp, I am drenched.

"I'm going back," I yell.

"No, you're not," I answer.

My voice is lost in the wind and the rain.

"All right, all right—I am going to Rutterburg, Vermont," I sing out, lifting my voice above the sound of the rain. A rumble of thunder answers me—the gods are listening—and I press my back against the tree and I feel stronger suddenly, as if I am part of it all, part of the tree and part of the storm, part of the thunder and part of the rain. I lift my face and the rain pours down. And I begin to sing:

> *The farmer in the dell,*
> *The farmer in the dell . . .*

T: So. We have arrived at the point where your
        suspicions were aroused.

A: I don't remember arriving at that point.

T: Are you playing games?

A: No. Why should I play games? I'm on the
        edge of panic half the time. Why should I
        play games?
        (5-second interval.)

T: Forgive me. If I seem—abrupt, critical—it is only for your sake.

A: I know.

(7-second interval.)

T: Let me refresh your memory. At the last meeting, you mentioned the telephone call from Amy, from her father's office. The visiting editor from Rawlings. Did that arouse your suspicions?

A: It made me feel—funny.

T: How do you mean, "funny"?

A: Well, what Amy said about there being no Farmers, no Farmer family, in Rawlings. And even the way I had tried to cover up. As if I had to cover up, instinctively. As if I knew something was wrong.

T: And what did you think was wrong?

A: I didn't know.

T: Did you think your father had been lying to you all that time? That you and your family didn't come from Rawlings?

A: No. I couldn't allow myself to think that and yet I kept getting these funny feelings— remembering that night we ran away. That seemed to be mixed up with it all.

T: Did you confront your father?

A: No. I couldn't do that. But I felt that I could probably find out some other way.

T: What other way?

A: Oh, it was vague. Maybe look in old picture albums, old papers and letters, for some proof that we actually lived in Rawlings, that I'd been born there. And yet, it wasn't that pressing. I mean—I wasn't really in a panic.

T: It did not bother you too much, then?

A: Yes, it did. But only when I took the time to think about it. I was busy with school. With Amy and her Numbers.

T: You did not mention the visiting editor and your doubts about Rawlings to your mother or father?

A: No.

T: That seems like the most natural course you could have taken.

A: Maybe. But I didn't want to.
   (8-second interval.)

T: But you finally did something about it, didn't you?

A: Did I?
   (5-second interval.)

T: Yes, because otherwise we wouldn't be sitting here talking about it, would we? You would not have brought up Amy's telephone call at all, would you?

A: I guess not.

T: So tell me. What did you do about it?
   (5-second interval.)

T: Tell me.

A: I can't remember exactly.
   (15-second interval.)

But, of course, he did remember, finally. It was all clear and lucid now, unforgettable. He knew that his father kept his private and official papers in the bottom drawer of the desk in the den. An insurance agent required a desk at home, where he could fill out the never-ending series of reports and keep the documents and the other paraphernalia of his trade. Adam knew that the bottom drawer contained certain certificates that were taken out only on special occasions. Like the time he needed a birth certificate to show that he was old enough to join the Boy Scouts. (Adam dropped out after a few meetings—he wasn't interested in standing at attention, tying knots, or going on hikes.) Ordinarily, his father locked the drawer. The key hung on his key chain, along with the house keys and car keys and some others. His father always tossed the chain casually on an end table near the front door when he came into the house. Adam waited for his opportunity.

Actually, he was barely conscious of his desire to check the bottom drawer. He had become convinced that the visiting editor had made a mistake. Amy had never mentioned his visit again. Looking at his father in his proper suit and tie, Adam was ashamed of his suspicions. In fact, what suspicions, really? And yet that day when he saw the key chain on the table, and knowing that his father was out mowing the lawn, Adam knew that he would look into the bottom drawer. He picked up the key chain; the keys were cool to his touch. He could hear the lawn mower at the far end of the front lawn. Perfect. His mother was upstairs. She was always upstairs these days. She came down to prepare the meals and do the housework but increasingly she stayed in her room. At any rate, his father's desk was located in a spot from which he could observe the steps going upstairs.

Keeping his mind blank and his motives muffled, Adam walked to the desk, inserted the small key into the drawer lock, turned it, and pulled the drawer open. The drawer contained a dozen or so brown envelopes. Adam lifted out a few. The envelopes were identified with his father's familiar scrawl: *Mortgage. U.S. Treasury Bonds. New England Tel. And Tel. Stocks. Birth Certificates.*

He opened this last envelope and took out the three crisp sheets of paper inside. They were official looking, a blue seal at the bottom. Signed by Tobias Simpson, Town Clerk, Rawlings, Pa. Adam inspected the certificate that bore his name: Adam David Farmer. "We gave you my name as your middle name," his father had explained long ago, "because two Davids would confuse everyone." Adam inspected the certificate—and it all checked out. His birthday, February 14. Valentine's Day. His mother was sentimental about birthdays and Adam's in particular. She shopped for days and always baked a special cake. "A lovely day to be born, Adam, a day of love and tenderness," she said. He looked at his father's and mother's birth certificates. Same official-looking paper, same signature: Tobias Simpson, Town Clerk.

Adam flicked through the other envelopes. Insurance policies. Social Security cards. He looked at his card and his number. It was new-looking, fresh, untouched. Why would someone his age need a Social Security number? Suspicion made him pause and in that pause, the sound of the lawn mower grew louder, and Adam held his breath. The lawn mower's motor receded and Adam exhaled. He remembered that you needed a Social Security number to open a bank account and his parents had presented him with his own bankbook and $50 deposited in his name on his tenth birthday. There was only one envelope left in the drawer. It was sealed. Adam held it in his hand, the envelope almost weightless. He knew that he could not risk opening it. And he also knew that it probably contained nothing suspicious at all. In fact, he felt ridiculous and guilty investigating the contents of the drawer.

Still curious, he held the envelope up to the light and could see faint outlines of a document inside. The document looked familiar: the blue seal at the bottom. He realized that the envelope contained another birth certificate or something similar. The blue seal was identical to the seal on the other birth certificates. Why another certificate? Had someone else been born that he knew nothing about? Did he have an unknown brother or sister maybe? This was crazy, this was ridiculous. It could all be explained easily. But he had to open this envelope. He had to find out. He had to know.

He inspected the envelope. Plain, white, undistinguished. Like any other envelope he'd often seen on his father's desk. He searched the desk now, opening drawers, and came upon a bunch of white envelopes. He compared them with the sealed envelopes. They were the same. It would be easy . . .

The sound of the power mower suddenly died; an emptiness filled the air. Adam was too much committed to his search to stop now even though his father might be heading for the house for a glass of beer or to rest awhile. He quickly tore open the sealed envelope and withdrew the certificate. It was a birth certificate all right. Signed and sealed by that same Tobias Simpson, Town Clerk, Rawlings, Pa. At first, Adam thought the certificate was a duplicate of his own because his name was written on the paper: Adam David Farmer. But the date was different. This date was July 14. The year was correct, exactly as it appeared on the first birth certificate. But a different date. A different birthday. He had two birth certificates, two birthdays. Crazily, he thought, Was I born twice? And his hands began to tremble so badly that he could barely slip the certificate back into the envelope. His tongue was dry when he tried to lick the envelope. His hands shook as he replaced all the stuff in the drawer, turned the key in the lock, slipped the torn envelope into his pocket. He heard his father's footsteps at the back door as he returned the keys to the table. He went downstairs and hid in the cellar until the trembling stopped.

T: And what did you do about it?
A: Nothing. There was nothing I could do. I figured it was a mistake. I figured that when we left Rawlings, my father had arranged

for the birth certificates to be made out—
we'd need them wherever we were going—
and that the town clerk, that Tobias Simpson, had made a mistake and given him the
wrong one or something. Wrote down the
wrong date. And probably my father didn't
notice it until later and had to send back
for the right one.

T: But why this reaction of yours? You trembled, you shook, you had the shivers. You
hid in the cellar.
(8-second interval.)

A: That was my first reaction. Later I got myself under control and tried to be reasonable
about it all. There had to be a simple explanation. But—

T: But what?

A: But I wondered, Why did he keep the birth
certificate if it was wrong, had the wrong
date? And why did he keep it sealed?

T: What did you do about it?
(5-second interval.)

A: I'm tired. I've got a headache.

T: What did you do about it?

A: It's late. I want to go to bed.

T: What did you do about it?

A: I can't remember. It's too hazy.

T: What did you do about it?
(6-second interval.)

A: Nothing . . .

But he did do something. He became a spy, a secret agent in his own home, listening at doorways, eavesdropping on telephone conversations, watchful and wary and suspicious.

"What's the matter—don't you feel well?" his mother asked. She was always solicitous about him, concerned and worried, emerging from her sad cocoon to fuss over him.

"I'm all right, Mom," he answered.

But he would study his mother, even though she was so sweet and innocent that he felt guilty for his doubts. He wondered what secrets she harbored, what dark knowledge she kept hidden within her. Is this what made her sad, what kept her in her room during the day, closeted in the house all the time, seldom venturing into the outside world? And his father—what about his father? In his proper clothes, his suit and vest, his morning newspaper. What secrets lurked in him? Or am I dramatizing, Adam wondered. He wanted to be a writer, to capture drama on paper. Was he really manufacturing mysteries to satisfy his literary longings, finding mysteries where they did not in fact exist?

Although Amy was the most important person in his life, he couldn't bring himself to talk to her about the doubts that tormented him. He was afraid she would laugh. He was afraid to lessen himself in her eyes. She had brought brightness and gaiety to his life and he didn't want to risk losing it all. That's why he submitted to the Numbers, accompanying her on those heady and hilarious but somehow terrible trips to the A&P and the Holiday Inn. When he thought of telling her what was bothering him and anticipating her reaction—Amy who never took anything seriously—he drew back and remained silent. A tortured silence. And he continued to spy, to probe, to watch . . .

T: And what did you find out, finally?
A: Too much. And not enough.
T: Do you really believe that or are you merely being clever?
    (5-second interval.)

T: I am sorry to be so blunt. Please explain what you mean.

A: I wasn't trying to be a wise guy. I was telling the truth. I found out, for instance, about my mother's Thursday night telephone calls. And when I realized what the calls were all about, it was both too much and not enough. It was worse than just knowing about the birth certificates.

T: Tell me about the telephone calls.
(10-second interval.)

A: I have a feeling you already know about them. I have a feeling you know everything, even my blank spots.

T: Then, why should I make you go through it all? Why should I carry on this charade?

A: I don't know.

T: You disappoint me. Can't you think of the one person who will benefit?
(5-second interval.)

A: Me. Me. Me. That's what you said at the beginning. But I never asked for it. I never asked to benefit by it.
(4-second interval.)

A: I have a headache.

T: Don't retreat now. Don't retreat. Tell me about the phone calls your mother made.
(5-second interval.)

A: There really isn't very much to tell.

Actually, there was a lot to tell but he didn't want to speak anymore, he wanted only to say the minimum, to say the words that would satisfy Brint and then go back to his room, to rest and relax. He didn't want to pick up the burden of remembering any longer. He wanted to coast awhile, float, not let it matter, drift. This is why he hated Brint sometimes. Because he interrupted the sweet drifting. With his questions. His incessant, never-ending questions.

T: Tell me what there is to tell, whether it's very much or not.

A: I don't know if I want to talk about the call.

And yet there was something good in the talking, in the discoveries. He had learned that the talking *was* discovery, words would come to his tongue that he had not known were lying in wait for him. The facts of his life would appear the moment he told them. The empty spaces were filled, the terrifying blanknesses that loomed before him sometimes at night in the darkness and he'd wake up, not knowing who he was or where he was. In the talking, the blank spots were filled in.

T: What about your mother and the telephone calls?

A: The calls were made every Thursday . . .

Adam had been aware of the calls and not aware of them. He knew that Thursdays were his mother's best days. She was usually downstairs waiting for him when he got home from school. There was always the aroma of newly baked cookies or cake in the kitchen—something chocolate. Adam loved chocolate and on Thursdays his mother prepared a chocolate treat for him and watched with pleasure as he wolfed it down. Sometimes she hummed or sang as she worked around the house, dusting or mopping up. Early in the evening on Thursdays she would disappear into the bedroom, closing the door behind her. Adam was cautioned not to use the telephone at that hour. "Your mother's special telephone hour," his father explained a long time ago. Adam had accepted the explanation without question and the telephone hour became part of the fabric of the household. He figured that his mother had set aside this time of day to complete all her calls to friends (but what friends?), to relatives (they had no living relatives, his father had informed him with regret a long time ago), her committeewomen (his mother was too shy and withdrawn to be active in social or civic affairs). And yet the telephone hour had gone on for so long a time that Adam had never really questioned its purpose or reason. It belonged to the world of adults, and adults often did things, sometimes ridiculous, sometimes beyond comprehension, but they were allowed to do them simply because they were adults. They needed no other reason.

His suspicions aroused by the two birth certificates and the tantalizing problem they presented, Adam began to question the familiar, everyday events of his life, and the comings and goings of his mother and father. He watched for telltale clues, any remark or action that could not be explained. He listened avidly for any mention of Rawlings, Pennsylvania. None. The routine of their lives went on without incident, and Adam told himself that he was looking for trouble where none existed. He told himself that both the birth certificates and the strange stuff about Rawlings could be explained away.

One Thursday evening, his mother excused herself as usual and went upstairs to the bedroom, closing the door. His father went downstairs to the cellar; he had transformed part of the cellar into a combination recreation room and office, pine-paneled, with some office paraphernalia plus a Ping-Pong table and a television set. He and his father played Ping-Pong occasionally, but most of the time his father used the room for business purposes, writing reports and policies there and meeting once in a while with businessmen or insurance company officials. On that particular Thursday, with his mother upstairs and his father downstairs, Adam spotted the extension telephone hanging on the wall of the den. He drew a sharp breath. Holding the breath, he made his way across the room like a sleepwalker. He placed his hand on the telephone; the instrument was cool to his touch, and the coolness established reality, the reality of what he was about to do: eavesdrop on his mother. He thought of Amy's belief in mischief. He exhaled, letting the air seep out of his mouth, and then picked up the receiver, slowly, painstakingly.

He heard a voice he did not recognize. A soft

voice, cultured, more than cultured, detached, as if speaking from far away, not far away in distance but in something else. A woman's voice.

". . . it's beautiful here, Louise, this is the loveliest time of the year."

Then his mother's voice: "It must be so peaceful there, Martha, so safe, so secure."

"But it's not a retreat from the world," the voice answered, a gentle admonishment in the words. "It's not simply a place to hide, Louise. You know that. Otherwise, there would be no point in being here, would there?"

"Of course, of course," his mother said. "Only, when I think of all that's happened, I envy you, Martha."

"Enough of that, enough." The gentle chiding was there again. Although the woman's voice didn't disclose any evidence of great age, she spoke to Adam's mother as if she were much older and his mother a child.

"And now tell me, Louise, about Adam. How's my fine nephew doing? What has he been up to this week?"

That word hung in the air, isolated from the others. *Nephew.* And superimposed on the voice was his father's voice saying, a long time ago: "We're alone in the world, Adam—you and your mother and me. That's why you've got to grow up strong and brave and good. You're the last of the line and you've got to keep it going . . ." *Nephew.* He listened now in disbelief as his mother recounted his activities of the past week and it was as if she were speaking of someone else. She told of the math test for which he had received a *B*+; the English composition that Mr. Parker had asked him to read aloud to the class, bringing him both embarrassment and triumph; she told her what he ate, what he wore, the new shoes he had bought—all the trivialities of his life, with no mention of the things that mattered: Amy or the poetry he wrote late at night in his room, his longings, his hopes . . .

". . . he's such a good boy. I feel bad about what's happened . . ."

"Now, Louise, you're in a black mood tonight— please, cheer up a little . . ."

"I know, I know. We have so much to be thankful for—*I* have so much—David and Adam and, of course, you, dear Martha—"

A noise caught Adam's attention: his father's footsteps. He removed the receiver from his ear but realized he couldn't simply hang up—the click would echo like an explosion across the wires. The footsteps grew closer as his father came up the stairs. Adam excruciatingly watched his own hand, with the receiver in it, approach the instrument. He put the receiver in the cradle, softly, gently, with tenderness. And then whirled as his father walked into the den. Thankfully, his father was reading one of his insurance contracts as he walked along and did not notice Adam standing guiltily at the telephone. But more than that, he did not see the terrible look of astonishment that Adam knew was shining in his eyes.

They've been lying to me, he thought with horror. *All my life, they've been lying to me . . .*

T: And so, for the first time, you had actual
       and direct evidence that there was some-
       thing wrong, that something was askew.
       (5-second interval.)
T: Do you feel well?
A: I'm not sure. I feel—dizzy.
T: An anxiety reaction, nothing more. Oh, the
       dizziness is real, I grant you. But the cause
       is anxiety, the sudden sharp memory.
A: May I rest? I'm tired now.
T: Are you retreating?
A: No. Really. But I'm dizzy and tired and my
       stomach feels queasy. I feel as though I've
       been here, in this room, forever.
T: I agree, it has been a long session, the long-
       est thus far. More than an hour—almost
       two. Let us suspend then.
A: Thank you.

END TAPE OZK006

There are three of them.

They are huddled around a table in the corner near the jukebox, eating popcorn. They toss the popcorn in the air and catch it in their mouths as if they're on stage and expect people to applaud. The jukebox is old and decrepit, no neon lights, no fancy touches. I wonder if it has "The Farmer in the Dell" but that is impossible, of course. "The

Farmer in the Dell" is not a jukebox kind of song. I am worried about the three guys eating popcorn. They glance my way once in a while and then whisper among themselves.

This is a small restaurant, a lunchroom really, and we are the only occupants. The counterman is a small thin fellow with a toothpick sticking out of his mouth and he is always on the telephone. No sooner docs he hang up the phone but it rings again and the toothpick dances in his teeth as he talks.

The clam chowder is hot. It burns the roof of my mouth and I take a gulp of water and then chew the small soda crackers. The chowder soothes my stomach and dissolves the rock there.

I look at the three guys and I am glad that my bicycle is at the police station. When I arrived in Carver a few minutes ago, the first building I saw on Main Street was a combination Post Office, Police Department, and Fire Department. I went inside and asked the policeman at the desk if I could leave my bike for safekeeping while I found a place to eat. He was reading a newspaper and didn't even look up. "Sure, kid," he said, "we aim to please." The weird thing is that he didn't look at me at all. I mean, I could have had two heads or been carrying a rifle or anything and he wouldn't have cared. I didn't leave my father's package with the bike. I untied the belt that held it to the bike and took it outside with me. On the street, I noticed that Carver is such a small town that it doesn't even have parking meters. I spotted the lunchroom—the faded sign said *Eats,* that's all. I like that kind of thing—Amy does, too—nothing phony or fancy about it.

The counterman ladled out the clam chowder while talking on the telephone. The telephone was cradled between his chin and shoulder. I figured the chowder would be good for sustenance on my journey, all that milk and stuff. The man dropped a huge chunk of butter into the chowder and grimaced at me. I realized the grimace was actually a smile. The butter immediately began to melt. I don't particularly like butter melting in my clam chowder but he seemed to think he was doing me a favor so I smiled and said "Thanks." He waved me away, still talking on the telephone, his voice so low I couldn't hear what he was saying.

Something hits my arm as I eat and I look down at the floor and see where the piece of popcorn has landed. Another piece arrives, barely missing the chowder. Like in school, when the wise guys threw spitballs. I don't look at the troublemakers and I concentrate on my chowder. I blow on the chowder to cool it off. I remove my father's package from the other chair at the table and put it on my lap. For safekeeping. I hear the popcorn guys giggle. You can tell them a mile away, the wise guys. I had recognized them as soon as I stepped into the place. They are everywhere in the world, in schools and offices, in theaters and factories, in stores and hospitals.

Now one of them gets up and walks toward me. He's about sixteen or seventeen and he has freckles and straight white teeth and he looks like a million other kids his age except for that subtle difference that marks him for what he is.

"Never saw you around here before, kid," he says, stopping at my table. Looming above me.

I take a spoonful of the chowder. It's getting cooler and I can swallow it without burning my throat.

"I'm just passing through," I say.

"Where you from?" he asks.

"Monument. In Massachusetts."

"And where are you going?"

He is asking questions but it's obvious that he is not interested in the answers. The questions are only a prelude to what he really wants: trouble.

"Rutterburg. Rutterburg, Vermont."

"You hitching?"

"No. I've got my bike."

All the time I'm talking, I'm gulping down the chowder and chewing the clams and the crackers.

"Well, where's your bike?"

He walks to the window and looks out into the street. He looks back at his friends who are still at the table tossing popcorn into their mouths and missing most of the time. "I don't see no bike."

"It's at the police station," I say. "I left it there for safekeeping."

I realize immediately I have made a mistake by saying that. He had been walking away from the window, toward my table, and now he stops in mid-motion. He shakes his head, as if tremendously puzzled. He looks again at his friends. "The police station?" he asks, in mock amazement. "To keep his bike safe?" I know what is coming. And it comes: "I guess he doesn't trust us," he says, shaking his head, his voice phonily sorrowful. "I guess this boy from Massachusetts don't trust the people in Carver, New Hampshire."

I swallow the last of the chowder and cram my mouth with crackers. My hand trembles as I put down the spoon. I should have taken my pills this morning. I look at the counter and the man is still on the telephone, the toothpick still in his teeth.

The wise guy hovers over me. "Is that the real reason you left your bike with the cops—because you don't trust us?"

"Look," I say, pushing away the bowl of chowder. "I'm on my way to Rutterburg and the bike is my only means of transportation. If somebody takes it, I'm dead."

"Can't you hitch?" he asks. "Hell, me and Dobbie and Lewis, we hitched all the way to Montpelier the other day. Right, fellas?" Glancing over his shoulder at them.

"Right, Whipper," one of them calls.

I wipe my lips with the napkin and pick up my father's package from my lap. My hands are shaking slightly.

"What's that?" Whipper asks.

"What's what?" I ask back, my voice quivering.

"That package there. In your hands," he says, impatient. "You're carrying it like it's a bomb or something. So careful. Have you got a bomb there? You planning to blow up Carver, New Hampshire?"

"No," I say. "It's a present. A gift. For my father. He's in Rutterburg, Vermont, and I'm bringing it to him."

I stand up, pushing the chair away. The legs of the chair scrape the floor. The other fellows stand up, too. My heart races: I am such a coward. The counterman is still on the telephone, turned sideways from us.

"I'd like to know what's in that package," Whipper says, his voice low and deadly.

We face each other. I realize now that he is shorter than I am but heavier. His shoulders are wide. There is a scar on his forehead above his right eye. His eyes are small, imbedded in his face. My heart is beating dangerously and I feel the blood rushing to my face.

"Yes sir, that package must really be something," he says. But he isn't looking at the package, he is looking at me. Our eyes are locked.

I clutch the package. I think of my father and I stand there, not moving. My heart is threatening to explode in my chest and my lungs scream with pain—I realize that I have been holding my breath —but I look him in the eye. The package is for my father and nobody, nobody is going to take it away from me or prevent me from bringing it to him. I stand there like a tree. I will not bend. I will not give him the package. I am the package.

Finally, he takes his eyes away from mine and steps back, a pitying look on his face.

"Shit on your old package," he says, shaking his head.

"Hey, what's going on there?" the counterman calls. Finally. He still hasn't hung up the telephone, it's still cradled on his shoulder, but at least he's become aware of what's been going on in his lunch-room.

"Aw, nothing, Luke," Whipper says and fades from my sight, going back to his cohorts at the table.

I exhale. Then I draw sweet air into my lungs. The air caresses them. My heart is still pounding dangerously but the beats are beginning to soften. I grab my father's package and I get out of there. Quick. Without looking right or left.

T: What's the matter? How can I be of assistance?
(5-second interval.)

T: What's wrong? Evidently, you are upset—
but tell me.
(10-second interval.)

T: I do not want to seem unnecessarily harsh

but it would assist the situation if you spoke,
if you explained.
(5-second interval.)

T: My boy, it is two fifteen in the morning. I
     told you at the beginning I would be avail-
     able to you at any time of day or night.
     And that is true. That is why I am here. But
     you must also do your part. You must as-
     sist me.
     (10-second interval.)

T: Tell me—what is wrong? Evidently, there is
     something wrong. What is it? I am here to
     help.
     (6-second interval.)

A: What comes next?

T: What do you mean?

A: You know what I mean.

T: Explain, please.

A: The blanks. All the blanks. If you know
     what they are, fill them in for me . . .

He had awakened from sleep as if shot out of a can-
non. Out of the everywhere into the here. And
now. The room, the bed, the cold moonlight chill-
ing the room. He was in the bed and aware of the
cold sheets but he was also suspended, isolated, in-
habitant of an unknown land, an unknown world
and he himself unidentified. Caught and suspended
in time. Who am I? I am Adam Farmer. But who
am I? I am Adam Farmer. But Adam Farmer was
only a name, words, a lesson he had learned here in
the cold room and in that other room with the

questions and answers. Who is Adam Farmer? He
didn't know. His name might as well have been
Kitchen Chair. Or Cellar Steps. Adam Farmer was
nothing—the void yawned ahead of him and behind
him, with no constant to guide himself by. Who
am I? Adam Farmer. Two words, that's all. He was
oozing perspiration, floating in his own body fluids,
the pajamas soaked with sweat. Lie still. Lie still,
lie still and the panic will pass. That's what they
told him and sometimes the panic passed. But only
with a pill and, some desperate nights, with a shot,
the needle bringing peace at last.

But now at this moment he was a raw wound,
bleeding panic, the bedsheet a shroud, crazy. He
tried to send his mind in different directions, past
and future, but it did not work. Faces passed by as
if on a whirling merry-go-round but they vanished
before he could focus on them, pin them down,
bring them into sharp portrayal.

There was a strange sound in the room. And he
listened, mouth agape, bones chilled. His own
sounds, a moan issuing from his body. He tried to
clutch at something in the dark, seeking something
to hold onto, but there was nothing. He was surrounded by nothingness, here in the bed and here
in his life. What life—whose life?

T: We have filled in many blanks. Or don't
      you remember?
A: Not enough. Not enough.
T: These things can't be rushed. You were told
      that in the beginning. You must relax. You

must ride out these panics. I am as much in a hurry as you to fill the blanks but it's a time-consuming thing.

A: Why can't I remember? Why can I remember just so much, a little at a time?

T: Do you suppose it's because you really don't want to remember?

A: But I do, I do.

T: Perhaps one part of you wants to remember and another part doesn't.

A: But why?

T: Who knows?

A: Is it because there's something so terrible there that one part of me doesn't want to know about it?

T: That's what we must learn. Slowly and patiently.
(10-second interval.)

T: It is late—do you wish something to make you sleep? To ease, as you call it, the panic?

A: I'm tired of pills and needles.

T: Perhaps that's a good sign.

A: Why do you have so many "perhapses" and "maybes" and "we'll sees"? Can't you help me?

T: This is the best way I can help you.

A: It isn't enough.

T: Should we review, then? Review all you have remembered? All the blanks that have been filled?

A: No. I don't care about the blanks that are filled in. It's the ones that are still blanks that I want to talk about. What am I doing here? How long have I been here? I hate this place. The people here hate me, too.

T: Why should they hate you?

A: They know I'm not like them. That's why they hate me.

T: Tell me, how do you know they hate you?

A: I know. I know.

T: But how?

(5-second interval.)

A: I'm tired now.

T: Is the panic gone?

A: Yes, I think I can sleep now. Without the pills.

T: You may have one if you wish.

A: Well, maybe one.

T: Fine. Fine. We shall meet again in only a few hours.

A: Good. I'm really sleepy.

T: Sleep well, sleep well.

A: Thank you.

END TAPE OZK007

I am about to get on my bike and leave the town of Carver forever when I spot the telephone booth down the street. At last. I lash my father's package to the basket and push the bike toward the booth. An old lady looks at me as I go by and she smiles at the *took* on my head. She has a hat on her head, too. It looks like a red flowerpot. Complete with flowers. I smile at her. I am happy suddenly. I will survive Carver and next comes Fleming and then Hookset and Belton Falls. There are long distances between Fleming and Hookset and then between Hookset and Belton Falls but this does not discourage me. I feel strong and resolute. I defeated the troublemakers in the lunchroom and I will defeat anyone else. But most of all, I am about to talk to Amy, to hear her voice again.

I fumble for change and insert the coin and the male operator comes on the line. I give him the number and go through all the rest of the routine and then the line is ringing, ringing. Please be home, Amy, please be home.

"Hello, hello."

The voice is harsh and impatient: Mr. Hertz's headline voice.

"Hello, may I speak to Amy?"

"Who is this?"

"Adam. Adam Farmer. I'd like to speak to Amy, please."

"Amy who? There's no Amy here."

The voice is not the headline voice of Mr. Hertz, after all. This is not her father.

I see the three fellows from the lunchroom on the street. They are drifting in my direction. Two of them are walking side by side, slowly and leisurely but something threatening in their pace. The other one, Whipper, walks alone, ahead of them. I feel trapped in the booth. The bike is vulnerable, untied and unbolted outside the booth. And I have a wrong number.

"Listen," the man on the phone begins, "I've got the bug and I been hacking away all day and I finally doze off and then the phone rings . . ."

"I'm sorry," I say.

And I slam down the phone. I don't like to hang up on people but the troublemakers are drifting closer and I have to get out of there. I'm sorry, Amy. I can't even get a telephone number right. I don't deserve you.

The boys are coming closer, slowly but surely and menacingly, and I swing open the door of the booth and grab the bike. I run along beside the bike and then leap upon it. My feet engage the pedals and I pump away. I shoot through a red light and a car blows its horn at me but I am away, leaving Carver behind, leaving the troublemakers behind, but I don't feel brave anymore and my cheeks are wet even though it isn't raining.

TAPE OZK008   0930   date deleted T-A

A: The gray man.

T: One moment please. Let me sit, first.

A: The gray man.

T: You look positively excited. I have never seen you in such a state. This is good.

A: The gray man.

T: And who is this gray man?

A: I'm not sure. But he's important. It

happened last night after I returned to my room. They gave me a pill. And I lay there, letting myself drift. Thinking of all the blank spots that have been filled in— Amy—the clues—and suddenly I remembered him.

T: And you call this person the gray man?

A: Yes. But only in my mind. That's what I always called him. The gray man.

T: And why was that?

A: I don't know. I'm not sure. But I think it's important. He's important.

T: In what way?

A: I can't tell yet. I'm not certain. But I think of him, what he looked like, and I know he's important, a real clue. I can feel it in my bones.

T: Tell me more.
(3-second interval.)

A: I wish I could. But I can't.

T: Can't or won't?

A: Can't, won't? Don't you think I want to remember, that I want to know? All I know right now is that there was a man in the past, someone I referred to as the gray man, and I have a feeling he was important. In all that blankness, he's the only clue I've got.

T: Then rest easy, relax, let it come. Perhaps a pill . . .

A: No, no pill. No shot, either.

T: Whatever you wish.
       (*10-second interval.*)
T: Anything?
A: Nothing.
T: Don't force, don't force. Let the thoughts
       come. Try to think of this gray man, what
       he looked like, what his name was, what
       he did, where did you see him most of the
       time, was he a friend, a relative, an uncle,
       perhaps—
A: Shut up, stop.
       (*10-second interval.*)
A: He's gone. I had him—I had him right on
       the brink—I almost remembered and now
       he's gone.
       (*5-second interval.*)
T: He'll return. The important thing is that
       you made contact. Remember earlier?
       How the clue of the dog led to the clue of
       Amy Hertz and that phone call. And the
       phone call led to the birth certificates—
A: I don't want to talk about all that. I want to
       go back to my room.
T: There is no hurry.
A: I'd prefer to go back.
T: Let us talk of something else.
A: I want to go to my room.
       (*10-second interval.*)
T: For instance, Paul Delmonte—
A: Is he the gray man?
T: Do you think he is?

A: I don't know. You asked me about him before. At the beginning. And I said I didn't want to talk about him. But I was bluffing. I didn't know who he was.

T: Do you know who he is now?

A: No.

T: Who do you think he is?

A: I want to go back. I'm not going to say another word.

         (5-second interval.)

T: As you wish. Let us suspend.

END TAPE OZK008

I am a mile or so outside of Carver on a narrow
road in the country, no houses anywhere. Once
in a while a car passes, uncomfortably close on the
narrow roadway. The road is paved but it's pock-
marked with ruts and holes. The road drops off
into a ditch about four feet deep and there is no
sandy shoulder. I have no rearview mirror and I
try to maintain a straight course as I pedal along.
I am glad to be leaving Carver behind and glad for

the bike and glad for the sun shining and glad to be safely away from the wise guys, the trouble-makers. I am only sad about Amy but I will call her the next time I see a phone booth, before I eat or stash my bike or anything else. She is more important to me than food, than the bike even.

I hear a car coming.

The cars usually don't speed on this road be-cause it's not built for speed and there is barely room for two cars to pass each other. But this car that's approaching is going fast. I can tell by the motor. The motor roars and whines. The motor grows louder. I grip the handlebars tightly, holding on. I am afraid that the car will cause a rush of wind that will suck me off the road as it passes.

The car approaches, the sound of the motor gathering in volume, filling the air. It soars past me, at great speed, so close that it almost brushes my elbow. I am thrown off balance and lose speed and the bike almost tips over as the front wheel wobbles. The car recedes ahead of me and I want to raise my fist and hurl an insult at the driver but I look up and see a familiar face in the rear window of the car. One of the troublemakers at the lunch-room.

I pedal furiously now, not because I want to catch up with them but because this road is de-serted and I want to reach a better road or high-way as soon as possible. I feel more vulnerable than ever. There are no houses in sight. Most of the cars use the Interstate that runs parallel to this old road. I keep pedaling. There's a curve ahead.

Maybe there'll be a house or a new road or something around the curve.

I hear the car again. That unmistakable motor. The car is coming back. The car is rounding the curve, heading in my direction. The car's grille looks like the grinning mouth of some metal monster. The car is pink, a sickly pink, the kind of pink found in vomit. The car thunders by and I see the face of Whipper at the wheel and his grin is as evil and ferocious as the car's grille. The other two guys poke their heads out the window and laugh raucously as they go by.

I reach out and touch my father's package in the basket and I keep pedaling. There is nothing else to do but keep pedaling. I approach the curve and coast for a moment, anticipating rescue there. But there is nothing. Only open fields. Why do the ecologists think we are running out of space on this planet? I've seen so many unoccupied and uninhabited places today that I'm starting to feel lonesome for stores and houses and sidewalks and traffic jams. But now there is a panic in the loneliness. I know the car will come back.

The motor ignites the air again. I hear it coming.

The sound of the motor is louder now, as if magnified, as if the road is a tunnel with invisible walls and the thunder of the motor reverberates against those walls, increasing the decibels. I keep myself rigid, crouched on the bike, and the car comes closer, closer.

This time the car brushes me. I feel the wind,

like a monster's foul breath, and I feel the contact of metal and a whine as the metal strikes my bike. The bike is wobbling dangerously and I hang on. I fight to regain my balance. My shoulder bursts with pain and I realize that something has struck my shoulder. One of the guys in the car tried to hit me as the car went by. Now it's gone again. But it will come back. I know it will come back.

"God," I say and the word fills the emptiness left by the car, fractures the silence of the country air. I should have taken my pills this morning. I think of my options. I can leave the road and hide in the fields. But the fields present no hiding place. There are only a scattering of trees and I would be spotted right away. I would also have to abandon the bike. And I can't stay here either. The car will mow me down. I can only keep on riding, riding—hoping a car will come along that I can flag down. Or maybe the wise guys are tired of the game, maybe they won't come back after all. Maybe they realize what they're doing and it's against the law: assault with a dangerous weapon. They have turned the car into a weapon.

I hear the car coming again. Not toward me as I expected.

The motor whines. From behind me.

I hang on. I pedal furiously to maintain balance. I gather speed and momentum. My legs hurt and my arms hurt and my body hurts but I keep pedaling, hurried by the sound of the motor like a wind blowing me along. I hear the squeal of the car's tires and the whine of the motor and it's coming,

coming, louder and louder, powerful and undeniable, and I brace myself.

The car brushes by and hands reach out for me, pushing, grabbing, and I lose my balance, the bike wavers under me and heads for the ditch, the steep ravine by the side of the road, and I am helpless to halt its progress toward the ditch, and the wheels spin and I hear raucous laughter as I loom at the edge of the ditch and then feel myself falling, spinning, sucked into the ditch, sucked into the wetness and darkness of a sudden startling night-time.

T: Are you feeling better? They say you
        refused to get out of bed yesterday. Are you
        better today?
        (10-second interval.)
T: They say you have not eaten. That you
        have not slept. That you lie there staring
        into space.
        (5-second interval.)

T: But we know that you are not merely lying there staring into space, don't we? You are thinking, aren't you? Remembering?
(15-second interval.)

T: And much of what you are remembering is unpleasant, isn't it? Terrible. But I am here to help you make it not so terrible.
(10-second interval.)

T: You must allow me to help you get through this. You must not withdraw.
(10-second interval.)

T: You must stay with us—you must not retreat—
(5-second interval.)

T: You must face the gray man. Otherwise everything will come to a halt.
(10-second interval.)

T: We shall try later. Please—take the medicine. Food, at least. I am here, always, to help you. Remember that.

END TAPE OZK009

TAPE OZK010   0900   date deleted T-A

T: And how are we this morning? Forgive my
       cheerfulness but it's a beautiful day outside.
       The birds are singing. It is quite a
       beautiful day.
       (10-second interval.)
T: You look alert this morning. Eyes bright.
       Flesh tones normal. How do you feel?
       (10-second interval.)

T: They tell me you have eaten. Breakfast, at least. That's good. You must keep up your strength.
(10-second interval.)

T: Do you wish to converse? We can speak about anything you wish. I leave it up to you.
(5-second interval.)

T: There is no need to discuss the gray man. Unless you wish to. We can talk about anything at all, anything.
(5-second interval.)

T: Very well. We can suspend. There may come a time when you wish to speak to me and I may not be here.
(10-second interval.)

T: Let us suspend then.
(10-second interval.)

T: Suspend.

END TAPE OZK010

"You all right, son?"

I hear the voice and see the face at the same time as I rise from the spiraling darkness where there was nothing to hold onto and I wanted to scream with panic but could not and now suddenly *You all right, son?* and the panic is over and the face above me is kind and concerned, an old face, a grandfather kind of face.

"I'm all right," I say, struggling up. I don't like to be flat on my back—I always sleep on my stomach—and I don't like to be confined or held down. My instinct, then, is to get up on my feet, flailing my arms at anything that might try to hold me down, confine me.

"Take it easy, son," the man says, still gentle, still calm.

I nod my head, stalling, trying to establish myself in the world again. My arms ache and my mouth tastes metallic, like dirt and acid mixed together.

"You must have had quite a tumble," the man says.

I stand erect and the world settles down around me and I remember what happened—the trouble-makers and the car and the plunge into the ditch.

"Is the bike all right?" I ask.

"Seems okay," the man says.

We are standing by the side of the road. The man's car, a big station wagon with paneling, is parked nearby. A white-haired woman sits in the car, a worried expression on her face.

"Is he all right, Arnold?" she calls.

"Yes, he is, Edna," he answers. Then to me: "Sure you're okay? Boy, I was coming along slow, the wife doesn't like to go fast since she had her stroke, and I saw one of the wheels of your bike sticking up out of that ditch and we stopped and I came over to look, although the wife says people should mind their own business. You were lying in the ditch like you was fast asleep. I pulled your bike all the way up and then your eyes fluttered and you came to."

I nod, thinking of the wise guys. I look around, wondering if they might return. I wonder how long I've been unconscious in the ditch.

"What time is it?" I ask. My head aches.

"Coming up to four o'clock," the man says, his voice a Yankee twang, like a violin string being tuned.

"Thanks for stopping," I say. "I appreciate it. I guess I lost my balance on the bike and fell into the ditch."

"No broken bones?" he asks.

I flex my arms and pat my chest and thighs.

"No broken bones," I say.

"You from around here?" he asks.

"We're going to be late, Arnold," his wife calls.

"One minute, dear," he says, raising his voice. And again to me: "Can we give you a lift, son? We're going up to Hookset. You look kind of tired."

"Hookset, that's right next to Belton Falls, isn't it?"

"Only a mile or two."

I know that I have been determined to cover the distance by bike but it's almost four o'clock and I'll never make Belton Falls before darkness at this rate.

"Listen, we can throw your bike in the back of the wagon. And don't mind my lady. She hasn't been herself since the stroke. Got no patience, poor thing. But she's a fine lady."

I realize that the important thing is to reach

Rutterburg as soon as possible and not the manner of traveling.

"Well, if you don't think your wife will mind . . ." I say.

"You come with us. How far did you say you're going?"

"I'm going to Rutterburg, Vermont, but I'll be satisfied to make Belton Falls tonight. There's a motel there I can stay at and then arrive fresh in Rutterburg tomorrow morning."

"Well, you come along," he says. "We can take you as far as Hookset, and Belton Falls is just next door. I'd take you all the way but my lady has an appointment at the doctor's."

I push the bike toward the car and my legs resist movement. They echo with pain, my arms throbbing, my calves pulsing. I am a sheet of pain but the car awaits and I can rest and let my body renew itself.

"Don't mind my lady," the man says. "She's not herself these days."

I climb into the back seat of the car after putting the bike into the back of the station wagon. The woman darts a quick look at me and sniffs, her face pinched, her nose wrinkled. The smell of liniment fills the air, not locker-room liniment but sickroom liniment.

"I'm not very comfortable with strangers in my car, Arnold," she says. And the man shakes his head and murmurs, "Now, Edna, poor boy's had a fall and needs a ride. That's all."

The car bumps along, slow, about twenty miles an hour, and speeds up a bit once going up a hill, and the woman says, "Not too fast, Arnold, not too fast."

I close my eyes and let the minutes pass, let myself coast, let my body relax. I begin to feel nauseous. I have never been carsick in my life but now my stomach bounces with the movement of the car and I am afraid I will have to vomit. I look out the window at the passing scene. We are entering a town: Fleming, probably. That is my next stop and I think that maybe I should get out in Fleming and get some Alka-Seltzer in a drugstore. But I think of pedaling all the way from Fleming to Hookset and I tell myself, Hold on, hold on.

I begin to sing to myself, silently so that the man and woman won't hear me:

> *The farmer in the dell,*
> *The farmer in the dell,*
> *Heigh-ho, the merry-o,*
> *The farmer in the dell . . .*

I sing and I think of the motel waiting in Belton Falls and how a good night's sleep will soothe my body and restore my energy and how tomorrow I will see my father in Rutterburg.

> *The wife takes the child*
> *The wife takes the child*
> *Heigh-ho, the merry-o,*
> *The wife takes the child . . .*

It is pleasant now, drifting and singing, my stomach not churning anymore and the car purring smoothly and then I hear the man say, "Well, we're here, son . . ."

I must have fallen off to sleep because we are on a busy street, traffic heavy, neon signs pulsing in the gathering dusk.

"Is this Hookset?" I ask, surprised at the quick passage of time.

"Do you think we'd lie?" the woman asks, sniffing again.

"Now, Edna," the man says.

He stops the car and I get ready to leave. I gather my package and the road map. My stomach is nauseous again but I figure I will go into the first drugstore I see and order an Alka-Seltzer. I open the door and the sounds of the city grow in my ears, as if someone has turned on the volume.

The man gets out of the car to help me with the bike and he says, "I hope you get there all right, boy. You look kind of green around the gills there. Better get some rest before moving on."

"Thank you," I say. "I appreciate it very much."

He pats me on the shoulder and goes back to the car and I look around for a drugstore. Despite my stomach, I am glad to be in Hookset because it is only a short distance now to Rutterburg, Vermont.

TAPE OZK011   0915   date deleted T-A

A: My arm hurts. My body hurts. All those
        needles.

T: I am sorry. I shall ask them to shift the
        area of penetration. You realize it was
        necessary, don't you? You retreated
        completely. We had to take drastic
        measures.

A: I know.

T: You do understand, then?

A: I don't understand anything, really. Why I'm here. How I got here.

T: That's what we're attempting to learn. That's why we are going through—all this. *(8-second interval.)*

T: It's possible that you went into retreat because you were getting close to remembering—and there will be pain in the remembering. You realize that, don't you? It's possible that the gray man represents the key and at the last moment you refused to use the key, afraid of what would be lurking beyond the door the key would open. *(5-second interval.)*

A: I know who the gray man is now. I think I know everything.

T: Everything?

A: I think so—

T: Then tell me. Get it out. Begin anywhere but tell it, expel it. Who was this gray man?

A: He was part of our lives and yet not part of it. He was always there, someone I took for granted. Let me explain it this way: My father told me about a mystery story a long time ago, it was called "The Invisible Man." Not the invisible man they made a movie out of but another one. It was a murder story, I guess. Anyway, the cops were all watching the street, waiting for the killer to arrive, to strike. And the killer did arrive but nobody saw him. Later on, they discovered that the killer was the mailman, he had calmly walked down the street and no one had noticed him because he was like part of the scenery. He was so commonplace that he was invisible. That's the way the gray man was in our lives.

T: How often did he enter your life?

A: He came to our house once or twice a month. All those years. Usually on the weekend, Saturdays mostly. He'd ring the bell and immediately my mother would go up to her room and my father and the gray man would go down to the cellar.

T: The cellar?

A: I thought I'd told you—there was a room down there my father had paneled, finished off as a sort of recreation room and office. He and the gray man would go down there. For about an hour maybe. I never went down there with them. Then the man would leave.

T: And why did you call him the gray man?

A: That's the funny thing—his name was Grey. At least, my father called him that. But he also seemed like a gray man to me.

T: And why was that? Was he addicted to gray clothes?

A: Not really. But there was something— gray about him. His hair was gray. But

more than that: to me, gray is a nothing
color and that's how Mr. Grey seemed to
me. Like nothing.

T: So, he came to your house all those years
and you were never curious about him
or suspicious?

A: Oh, there was nothing to be suspicious
about. My father had told me Mr. Grey was
supervisor of the New England branch of
the insurance company that employed him.
He said they had to draw up confidential
reports and such. And I accepted the
explanation, of course. I had no reason
to doubt my father back then. I mean,
Mr. Grey had been a presence in our lives,
part of the scenery, part of the house—
like the furniture. There was nothing to be
suspicious about, until I became suspicious
of everything.

T: And when did you become suspicious of
everything?

A: After that phone call, when I overheard
my mother talking to that woman who
was my aunt. A secret aunt. I could
overlook the two birth certificates. That
could have been some kind of mistake.
But not this woman. She was real.

T: Why didn't you confront your parents
about the woman?
(6-second interval.)

A: Because I was in a panic. Trying to
pretend it never happened, that I hadn't

heard the telephone call. I also knew that
I would have to confess how I'd spied on
my mother, listened in on her conversation.
I kept telling myself that there had to be
a logical explanation. I knew they loved
me and I had to trust their love, believe
in them. So I was in a panic and I felt
guilty and I found it hard to look either
my mother or my father in the face. And
then that particular Saturday arrived—

T: Tell me . . .

He had been waiting for a telephone call from
Amy Hertz. The night before she had told him
that she was planning a Number at St. Jude's
Church the following day. Something to do with
a wedding.

Adam had been appalled at the prospect, losing
the cool he always tried to display to Amy.

"Listen, Amy, you're not going to desecrate a
church, are you? Or invade somebody's wedding?"
he asked.

"Of course not, dear Ace. Merely a little diver-
sion. And don't worry. The church itself isn't
involved. The parking lot—that's our area of concentration." She refused to explain further. "I'll
call you in the morning. The wedding isn't until
two in the afternoon."

Thus he was hanging around the house, both
hoping for and dreading Amy's call, when Mr.
Grey rang the door bell. Adam opened the front
door. Mr. Grey looked as grim and bleak and—as

gray as usual. He seldom wasted time with polite greetings, murmuring "My boy" to Adam and entering the house briskly, as if being chased by the wind. Adam heard the bedroom door being closed by his mother upstairs. His father came forward from the back of the house. Years ago, Mr. Grey brought Adam occasional gifts—toy boats, bats, balls. Now he barely glanced at Adam.

Adam stepped aside. Mr. Grey and his father headed, as usual, for the cellar stairs. Adam watched them, curious about Mr. Grey for the first time. If he had an aunt somewhere out there hidden from him, could Mr. Grey be an uncle? He dismissed the thought as absurd.

Restless, bored, he prowled the rooms, waiting for Amy's call. He realized that more and more he had become dependent on Amy to fill his hours, to fill his life. Adam's shyness had always prevented him from making easy friendships. He wasn't capable of intimacy with others—he didn't dare confess his hopes and desires to others, his longing to be a famous writer. He thought people would either laugh or scoff. Strangely enough, Amy Hertz, whose goal in life seemed to be only laughter and mischief, had turned out to be the person with whom he was comfortable, with whom he could share his dreams. He kept few secrets from her. And he wondered sometimes if he should tell her about all his doubts—the birth certificates and now the secret aunt. He was afraid, of course, that she'd tell him he was losing his mind.

He thought of Mr. Grey in the recreation room

below. What a square, a stuffed shirt, he thought. He considered what a target Mr. Grey would make for one of Amy's numbers. Amy had driven Mr. Crandall, a hated teacher, up the wall a few weeks ago by sending him anonymous love letters, passionate letters obviously from a student. The Amy Hertz touch: giving the letters a definite masculine tone so that poor Mr. Crandall thought he was being pursued by a passionate teen-age homosexual.

I, too, am capable of mischief, Adam thought. And he went to the cellar door. He listened. Nothing. He opened the door and went down the stairs. The door to the recreation room was closed. Adam walked stealthily toward the door, almost on tiptoe. He placed his ear against it, listening shamelessly. Nothing. The place must be soundproof, he thought. It struck him then that the recreation room was almost like a vault; he had always felt mildly claustrophic in the room. His father had sealed off the cellar windows, completely paneling the walls and ceilings. "When I want privacy, I get privacy," he had joked. But had he really been joking?

Adam's ear was warm against the wood of the door.

At that moment, he heard the knob turn.

Adam swiveled around and withdrew into the shadows.

His father emerged, in silhouette. Adam flattened himself against the wall. Had his father seen him? Had he heard him outside the door?

His father paused now, said something to Mr. Grey that Adam was too flustered to hear—his heart beating loudly in his body—and crossed the cellar. He went up the steps.

Adam heard him proceed through the rooms upstairs, his steps echoing in the ceiling. There was no sound from Mr. Grey in the recreation room. Adam was afraid that the thud of his heart could be heard, like the heart in that Edgar Allan Poe story. His father came back down the stairs. He did not look in Adam's direction. He didn't seem upset or rushed. He closed the door, shutting out the ray of light. And Adam allowed himself to relax, to sag against the wall. He was drenched with perspiration. He made his way slowly and quietly up the stairs.

T: Is that all?

A: No.

T: Take your time, now. I see you are perspiring. There are Kleenexes there. Help yourself.

A: Thank you.
       (*10-second interval.*)

T: And had your father seen you at the door downstairs?

A: Yes. But I didn't know that right away. I suspected that he had. When he and Mr. Grey finally came upstairs from the cellar, my father glanced at me in a strange way, suspicious. But he didn't say anything. I

found that I didn't want to confront him.
I told my father I was going to Amy
Hertz's house. But I didn't leave. I went
out to the garage and sat there on the
workbench. I was in a panic. I was in a
panic because I'm not built for subterfuge
and deception. I sat there feeling terrible,
ashamed of myself for spying on my
parents. I knew they loved me, that there
was a logical explanation for everything.
So I went back in the house, looking for my
father. To apologize. He wasn't in sight.
I looked through the downstairs rooms.
He wasn't there. I went upstairs. The door
to their bedroom was still closed. I
approached the door, intending to knock
and then go inside and make a clean breast
of everything I had done. Then I heard
their voices. And that changed everything.
Forever.
(10-second interval.)

T: And what did you hear?

A: It's funny. It was like that frantic
whispering on that night long ago. I heard
my father's voice. He was saying, "He's
becoming suspicious—he was listening at
the cellar door. He was trying to hear what
Thompson and I were saying." For a
minute, I thought he was talking about
someone else altogether, another situation
altogether, and I was relieved. I didn't

know any Thompson. Then I heard my
mother say, "He should stop coming here.
And he should use his own name in the
first place. Grey—Thompson—all these
years we called him Grey and now he's
someone else. These ridiculous games he
plays . . ." There was anger in my mother's
voice. I had never heard anger there before.
My father said, "He's probably got a
thousand names—that's how he survives.
That's what helps us to survive." And my
mother said, with the anger gone now and
the old sadness in her voice again, "That's
just what we're doing: surviving, not
living."
(7-second interval.)

T: Go ahead. Use the Kleenex again.
(12-second interval.)

A: Then my father said, "We have to do
something, Louise. He isn't a child
anymore. Didn't you say you thought he
might have been listening the other night
when you talked with Martha?" I didn't
hear her reply. And then I heard my father
say, "No matter what Grey—Thompson—
says, it's time to do something about
Adam." And I shivered there in the
hallway . . .
(8-second interval.)

T: It's all clear now, isn't it?
A: Yes.

T: Do you wish to rest awhile or do you want
to go on with it?

A: Let's go on with it.

TAPE CHANGE:
END OZK011

START:
TAPE OZK012   1019   date deleted T-A

A: Next thing I knew I was downstairs in the
recreation room, sitting there. I left the
door open. I knew that my father would
find me there eventually. I heard the
phone ring but I didn't bother answering
it although there was an extension in the
room. I sat there, as if in a trance. I knew
it was Amy on the phone. But Amy
didn't matter at the moment. I sat there
and waited for my father to come
downstairs and I don't know how much
time had passed . . .

He hadn't bothered to put on the lights. But a
feeble shaft of light penetrated the room from the
other part of the cellar and it struck a Ping-Pong
ball. The ball lay suspended in the darkness like
a miniature moon. He didn't know how long he
had sat there, and then he heard his father's voice.

"Adam?"

His father calling from the top of the stairs.

"Adam, are you down there?"

Adam didn't answer. His father must have

sensed his presence, however, because he began to descend the steps, blocking out part of the brightness that spilled in from the cellar outside the recreation room. His father advanced to the door of the paneled room and saw him.

"What are you doing down here?" he asked. "Amy called awhile ago and I told her you were on the way to her house."

He looked up at his father. His good father, that worried look on his face. Whatever had happened, he trusted him completely. But Adam still didn't speak. He didn't trust himself to speak, afraid of the words that might spill out of him, the questions he didn't want to ask, the answers he didn't want to hear. But at the same time, he wanted to know, he wanted to know everything. He was tired of pretending that nothing had happened, that the second birth certificate didn't exist, that he had not listened to that phone call. He was tired of faking it, being a fake.

"Are you okay, Adam?" his father asked, a frown of concern on his forehead. His father sat down beside him on the couch.

Adam looked at the Ping-Pong ball. It was no longer a moon, just a ball.

"What's the matter?" his father asked, voice light and bantering now, the same kind of voice he used with Adam's mother during her bad times.

Adam closed his eyes. And then without planning, without preliminaries, he said, "What's it all about, Dad? Who's Mr. Grey or is he Mr. Thompson? Who's that woman—Martha's her name—that Mom calls every week? What's going on, Dad?"

He knew that by asking the questions he was betraying himself, admitting that he had been spying and eavesdropping. And he also knew, deeply and sadly, that the answers would change his life, that there would be things in his life, in *their* lives, that he hadn't known before. Maybe that's why he had delayed the questions from the very beginning. Because he didn't want things to change. But the questions had been asked now. And he opened his eyes to confront his father.

"Jesus," his father said and Adam wasn't certain whether his father was swearing or praying. "Jesus," he said again, sighing, a long sigh, weariness in the sigh and sadness, too, such sadness.

His father touched his shoulder. A gentle touch, a caress, really. "How much do you know, Adam?"

"I'm not sure, Dad. Not very much." His voice sounded funny, an echo-chamber voice.

"Of course. I'm still not playing fair with you, asking that. You've suspected something for a while now, haven't you? I've seen you looking at me, at us, your mother and me, studying us. And lately you've been skulking around the house. Listening. Brooding. At first we thought it was Amy, that you were mooning about her. I tried to convince myself of that because I've always dreaded the day when you'd ask certain questions." He sighed again. "And now the day is here . . ."

"Are you going to tell me, Dad, what it's all about?" Adam asked. "I've got to know."

"Of course you have to know. It's your right to
know. You're not a child anymore. I've been telling myself that for a long time. But there never
seemed to be a good time for it . . .

T: And did he tell you?
A: Yes. Yes, he told me.
T: And what did he tell you?
A: That my name is Paul Delmonte, that there
      is no Adam Farmer.
      (*15-second interval.*)
T: Are you able to proceed?
A: Yes. I'm all right, I'm fine.
T: Then—what else did your father tell you?
A: Everything . . .

T: Everything?

A: Well, almost everything. That night I told
you about—the first memory—the bus.
I was right about that, my father said.
We *were* running away. Going to a new
place to live. And that day in the woods,
with the dog. We fled into the woods
because my father thought he had spotted
one of Them—

T: Who was Them?
        (9-second interval.)

A: I'm not sure. I think I knew once—maybe
        it will come back to me. But that day
        in the cellar my father told me who I was,
        who he was, who we all were. Suddenly
        I had a history, something I realized I had
        never had before. Everything changed in
        one afternoon, in that cellar, in a few
        hours . . .

His father's real name was Anthony Delmonte and he had been a reporter in a small town in upstate New York. The name of the town was Blount, population about 30,000. Famous for the high hills veined with granite that loomed above the town. Those hills drew a few Italians across the Atlantic a hundred years ago, men skilled in the uses of marble and granite, among them the grandfather of Adam's father. The quarries dried up after a while but the Italians remained and became assimilated into the town and the state. These were light-skinned, blond Italians from northern Italy. They grew no grapes on terraced slopes. Adam's grandfather was the first of his generation to seek an education; he graduated from law school and was modestly successful, conducting a law office in the heart of Blount. Adam's father did not seek a career in the law. He was drawn by the written word. He completed his studies at Columbia University in New York City and attended the Missouri Graduate School of Journalism. With his degrees tucked into his suitcase, he returned to Blount and became a reporter for the Blount *Telegrapher*. Soon he was promoted to staff reporter, then to political reporter. He loved working for the newspaper. He was intrigued by the power of words, not the literary words that filled the books in the library but the sharp, staccato words that went into the writing of news stories. Words that went for the jugular. Active verbs that danced and raced on the page. Roscoe Campbell, owner and editor of the *Telegrapher*, encouraged Adam's father to go beyond the superficial aspects of stories, to find the meanings below the surfaces, to root out what might be hidden or not apparent to the casual reader. He won the "Small City Reporter of the Year" award, presented annually by the Associated Press, for a series of stories involving corruption in Blount—an official in the Public Works Department involved in kickbacks connected with purchases of snowplows and trucks. Roscoe Campbell was delighted. Occasionally he allowed his award-winning reporter to spend a few days at the state capital in Albany. Once again, the owner beamed with pride—how many newspapers of similar size received exclusive stories from their own man at the State House?

Meanwhile, Adam's father and mother met and married. She was Louise Nolan, blue-eyed and dark-haired, a shy beauty, the younger daughter of tragic parents. Her mother had died giving birth to this second child, and her father, an artist of modest reputation in the Blount area, was seduced by beer, whiskey, rum or rye or whatever balm came in bottles. He froze to death one January night, having tumbled in a stupor to the snow-covered pavement of a back alley. The hard-working young reporter rescued Louise Nolan from her grief and they were eventually married in St. Joseph's Church, Adam's mother having been a devout Catholic all her life—religion, in fact, had always sustained her through bad periods, particularly after her father died. The wedding was modest and unpretentious; the parents of both were dead and they had only a scattering of distant relatives in that section of the state. After a honeymoon at Niagara Falls, they settled down in a five-room ranchhouse in Blount in the shadows of those hills that had drawn Adam's forebears to the town. Soon Adam was born, a sweet and docile child (Adam blushed at his father's description of him), and life was good, life was fine . . .

T: Yes, yes. I see, I see—

A: You sound impatient. I'm sorry. Am I going into too much detail? I thought you wanted me to discover everything about myself.

T: Yes, of course I do. I apologize for my seeming impatience. We have such a long way to go together.
(*5-second interval.*)

A: What do you really want to know about me? What's this questioning really about?

T: Must we discuss motive again? We have

agreed that these sessions are journeys to discover your past. And I am willing to serve as your guide.

A: But I sometimes wonder what's more important—what I find out about myself or what you find out about me.

T: You must avoid these needless doubts— they only delay the process of discovery and you are then left with those terrifying blanks.
(6-second interval.)

A: All right, then. I'm sorry. Guide me, like you said you would.

T: Then let us get on with it. Let's explore what happened to send your family from that idyllic existence in Blount out into the night on that bus . . .

He could still remember his father's voice in the cellar that day, and the Ping-Pong ball like a small planet suspended in space, his father's voice holding him captive, enthralled—and yet a small part of him was isolated and alone, a part that was not Adam Farmer any longer but Paul Delmonte. I am Paul Delmonte, a voice whispered inside of him. Paul Del-mon-tee. Then who is Adam Farmer? Where did he come from? And, finally, his father told him that Adam Farmer had come into being a long time before, when the reporter who was Anthony Delmonte—and would someday be David Farmer—had uncovered certain documents, obtained certain information at the State

House in Albany, information that would change
a lot of lives irrevocably . . .

T: What kind of information?

A: He wasn't precise about it. But I know
this much—it involved corruption in
government.

T: At what level of government—state,
federal?

A: Both. And there was more than government
involved. There were links.

T: What were these links?

A: Between crime—he spoke about the
organizations, the syndicates—and
government, from the local wards right
up to Washington, D.C.

T: Was he specific about these links?

A: Now you're sounding like an investigator
again—as if you're looking for specific
information that has nothing to do with
me as a person.

T: Everything has to do with you as a person.
We have to be specific. Haven't you dealt
in generalities, vaguenesses, long enough?
Lack of specifics—isn't that what gives
you nightmares at two o'clock in the
morning?
(5-second interval.)

A: I'm sorry. Anyway, he said the information
he found, information that took him a
year to uncover, made it necessary for him
to become a witness. To testify, in

Washington. Before a special Senate
committee. Behind closed doors. No
television cameras. No reporters. Later,
there would be indictments, arrests. But
the testimony had to be given in secret.
Otherwise—
Otherwise what?
I remember his exact words. He said that
otherwise his life wouldn't be worth a
plugged nickel. That was an expression
I had never heard before. But I knew what
it meant as soon as I heard it.
(*5-second interval.*)
Go on.
He went to Washington, he testified, he
gave evidence for investigators to follow
up on. They said he would be protected,
his identity kept secret. He trusted them.
He was away for almost a year, hiding
in hotel rooms, coming home once in a
while to visit my mother and me, while
guards stood around the house,
inconspicuous, in the shadows. I was
just a baby—two or three years old. He
said he was riddled with guilt during all
that time. But it was his duty, he said.
He said he was an old-fashioned citizen
who believed in doing the right thing for
his country, to provide as much information
as possible.

T: Earlier, you said that he told you *almost*
everything. What did you mean by that?

A: He said that there was a lot of information he couldn't give me. For my protection.

T: And how would this provide protection for you?

A: He said that if I was ever questioned about certain topics, certain information, I couldn't possibly give away the information if I didn't have it to begin with. He said I'd be able to pass lie-detector tests or any other tests. In other words, I could always tell the truth, even if some fancy truth serums were used, and I'd never betray anything.

T: What do you think you would have betrayed?
(6-second interval.)

A: That's a funny question.

T: In what way is this question of mine, as you say, funny?

A: It's as if your question about betrayal is trying to make me betray something. I don't know—I'm confused.

T: Of course, you're confused. May I make a suggestion? I suggest that this particular reasoning of yours, these doubts of yours, are a defense on your part. Whenever you are on the edge of revealing something important in your past, you stall, voicing suspicions of my questions because you are afraid, because you are reluctant to face your past.

A: I'm not afraid. I want to know.

T: Then let's go forward, not sideways, not backward.

A: All right . . .

(5-second interval.)

A: Where were we?

T: The testimony in Washington . . .

A: Well, finally it was over. He came back to Blount, returned to his job. Mr. Campbell had given my father a leave of absence. He thought he had been researching a book in Washington. The government had paid my father's salary. Anyway, it was all over. Done with. Indictments were issued. Quiet arrests made, sudden resignations in Washington. But no heroics—my father didn't want any. He only wanted to resume his life again, be with his family. And then it happened . . .

The bomb. Planted in the car. Waiting for his father to turn the key in the lock. But the explosion never occurred because a local policeman had observed two strangers lurking near the Delmonte household. A telephone call from police headquarters warned his father to stay in the house. A crew of bomb experts appeared at the scene and towed the car away. A later report disclosed that a bomb capable of destroying the car and everything within a ten-foot radius had been located, attached to the accelerator.

The next attempt came three nights later. His

father had worked late at the newspaper. He had felt nervous and edgy as he typed away but he refused to give in to his feeling of uneasiness. Anyway, there was a police officer on duty at the entrance of the building, assigned by the police chief at the insistence of Roscoe Campbell. His father finished writing—a three-part series on a possible scandal in the municipal purchasing department. No kickbacks this time but rental fees paid for equipment that did not, in fact, exist. His father walked down the stairs. The sight of the police officer provided a touch of comfort. The police officer turned toward him—a gun in his hand. His father froze. The gun was raised and his father saw the face, the expressionless eyes— the look of the hired killer, the hit man. A terrible sadness flooded him; he had let his wife down, his son—they would be left alone, abandoned. A pistol shot rang out, echoing as loudly as the detonation of a bomb. His father braced himself and then saw, in slow motion, the policeman crumpling up, mouth agape, eyes bulging from their sockets. He fell forward, the gun loosed from his hand, dropping to the sidewalk.

That was the night Mr. Grey entered their lives . . .

T: More specifics now, although you seem
        to dislike the word. Who, finally, was
        this Mr. Grey of yours? Until now,
        you have made him seem like a phantom
        flickering in and out of your lives.

A: He worked for the government, the federal government. My father said that Mr. Grey had been involved from the beginning, from the time my father first gave testimony. He'd been on the sidelines, watching, waiting . . .

T: A bodyguard?

A: No. More than a bodyguard. My father said he was one of the original men involved in a new government department.

T: What was this department?

A: Let me think a moment.
(5-second interval.)

A: I remember the title now—the U.S. Department of Re-Identification. It was supposed to protect people. To provide people with new identities. So that they could hide.

T: Hide from what?

A: From those they testified against.

T: I am afraid it is not entirely clear to me.

A: Let me try to remember exactly what my father told me.
(5-second interval.)

A: My head is beginning to hurt. To pound.

T: Do you wish a pill?

A: No. I don't trust pills anymore.

T: Does that mean you do not trust me anymore?

A: I'm not sure of anything right now—give me a minute to think—to think about all

the things my father told me—all the things
we talked about . . .

How they talked. Or, rather, his father talked and
Adam listened. But Adam also asked questions, a
hundred, a thousand it seemed. During those first
few days after the discovery of his identity and the
lives they led, he and his father talked incessantly,
the terrible silence finally broken. Sometimes they
talked in the paneled room in the cellar and at
other times outside, walking the streets, sitting in a
restaurant, lounging on a park bench. His father
explained why they covered so much territory. The
paneled room was a Safe Room; it had been
searched for "bugs"—listening devices—by Grey's
men and given clearance. If they didn't talk in that
room, it was best to conduct their conversations
while they were on the move, coming and going,
in public places, when the chances of being overheard or eavesdropped on were negligible. It was
during these conversations that his father brought
him up to date, told him how they had become
involved in this new life of theirs.

"In the final analysis," his father said, "we really
had no choice. Grey spelled out the options, the
alternatives. He had helped to develop the Department of Re-Identification. The department had
grown out of a sudden need as people began to
testify against organized crime. The first people to
give testimony were criminals themselves, members
of the organizations and syndicates who, for one

reason or another, decided to turn against their own kind. In exchange, they asked protection. The early cases were provided with bodyguards, nothing else. Some of the first witnesses were convicts and they had to be transferred to prisons where they couldn't be reached by the organizations. In some instances, new identities were created for witnesses who weren't in jail. They began new lives under assumed names."

Adam and his father were walking by a school-yard where some kids, mostly girls, were playing hopscotch and other games, their shouts and laughter innocent on the afternoon air. Adam suddenly felt like an alien.

"Grey explained the situation," his father continued, unaware of the children and the sunshine, head down, his eyes cruising the sidewalk. "My life as I had known it, he said, was ended. It was a matter of time before a bullet or a bomb or some other weapon finished me off. He had been my watchdog from the beginning. He and his men had alerted the police department when the bomb was placed in the car. One of Grey's men had shot the assassin who had impersonated the cop outside the newspaper office. Grey said that sooner or later the assassins would succeed. I couldn't be allowed to live—for a lot of reasons, the least of which was revenge. I had to be made an example to other people who might want to become witnesses. And they still didn't know how much I had really learned during the investigation, how much I could still tell the authorities. Or how much I knew then that wasn't worth much but might become important if later disclosures were made."

His father kicked at a stone, watched it roll into the gutter. "I'm not the hero type—I get scared too easily—but I tried to reason with Grey. I told him that I would take my chances, that this was still a free country, a country of laws, and that a citizen shouldn't have to go into hiding for his own protection. But Grey pointed out the clincher—he said that the bomb in the car hadn't been aimed at me alone but at whoever happened to be in the car when it exploded, and most likely that would be my family. He said that you and your mother weren't any safer than I was. Not as long as I continued to be Anthony Delmonte, resident of Blount, New York. I remained unconvinced—feeling that there was something wrong somehow with our entire system—until I returned home after Grey's visit with me at the office and learned that your mother had received a phone call. A simple and brief phone call in which someone quietly informed her that two funeral masses would be reserved in the next week at St. Joseph's Church. For her husband and son. Her punishment was that she would be allowed to live . . .

The sun had no right to be so bright, the shouts of the playing children so happy.

"That night, I called Grey, using a special number he had given me."

T: Thus, your family came under the
       protection of this Department of

Re-Identification.

A: Yes. But it was different in those days. My father said they were amateurs at that kind of thing. Today, there's an official Witness Re-Establishment Program—that's the official name now—with authority handed down by Congress. It's all smooth and cool and streamlined. Entire families are relocated, provided not only with new identities but with complete family histories, all documented, official. It's almost foolproof. But in those days the program was new. We were one of the first families involved. There was money enough—in fact, my father said a trust fund was established to finance my college education —but there were a lot of rough edges. Grey and his people had to improvise and sometimes they goofed.

T: How did they, as you say, "goof"?

A: Well, the birth certificates, for instance. When Mr. Grey brought us our new certificates, my birthdate had been changed from February 14 to July 14. Mr. Grey was furious, my father said. He wanted us to keep our original birthdates so there'd be less confusion, less chance of slipping up accidentally and giving the wrong date in the future. My mother was upset, too—she said a mother simply couldn't accept a change in the birthdate of her son. So Mr.

Grey arranged for another certificate.

T: But your father kept both, you said.

A: He was afraid of another goof, that the July 14 date might have become recorded somewhere and that I might need it in the future. So he didn't destroy it. He said it might have been a mistake on his part but that he, too, had to improvise in those days.

And the names. Adam could still hear his father's voice, a mixture of anger and disgust when he talked about their new names.

"Farmer, for God's sake. Grey and his bunch come up with Farmer. White, American, Protestant. WASP. And here I am Italian, and your mother Irish. And both of us Catholic, your mother a devout Catholic who never misses mass on Sunday or on holydays."

Grey resorted to more improvisation, suggesting that the Farmer family be converts to Catholicism. This meant baptismal certificates, confirmation papers.

"We were like puppets, you, your mother, and I," his father said. "As if we had no control over our lives. And we didn't, of course. Others pulled the strings and we jumped. Sometimes, I think someone with a terrible sense of humor was toying with us. Look at the name they selected for you— Adam. Somebody's whim, maybe. Adam: new birth, first man. I don't know. Your mother and I felt helpless but the thought of that bomb and that phone call made me go along. And so we found ourselves in Monument, Massachusetts."

T: Why Monument, why this city out of so
      many others?
A: You sound bored.
T: Please, no more judgments on me.
A: As if you've heard all this before and you're
      only going through the motions.
T: Time is too valuable to hear banal
      information repeated. If I knew why your
      Mr. Grey chose Monument as your new
      home, would there be any logical reason
      why I would ask you about it?
      (*10-second interval.*)
A: I guess you're right. As usual. As far as
      Monument was concerned, my mother
      insisted on staying somewhere in the
      Northeast, my father said. Mr. Grey agreed
      but not for sentimental reasons. He said
      it was a matter of life style, of blending in
      with our surroundings. We'd have been
      conspicuous, say, suddenly turning up in
      Texas. So Mr. Grey arranged for us to settle
      in Massachusetts. Actually, distance wasn't
      a problem, he said. Even without all the
      elaborate arrangements, there was little
      chance of anyone tracing us back to
      Blount . . .
T: What is the matter? You have suddenly
      grown pale.
      (*7-second interval.*)

A: Let me take it easy for a minute or two . . .
       (23-second interval.)
T: What has upset you?
A: Something I remembered as I was talking.
       The reason why Mr. Grey wasn't worried
       about anyone tracing us back to Blount . . .

The cellar again. With his father. His mother upstairs. His father reached inside his jacket and pulled out an envelope. A narrow manila envelope, slightly larger than letter size. He held the envelope in the palm of his hand for a moment, as if his hand were a scale and he was trying to determine its weight, its value, its importance. Finally, he unsealed the envelope, carefully lifting up the Scotch tape that crisscrossed it. He withdrew something that looked like a newspaper clipping. Yellowed, fragile. He handed it to Adam.

"This was the insurance Grey said he was providing us with," his father said, his voice filled with a bitterness Adam had never heard in his father's voice before.

Adam looked down at a five-column headline that preceded a long news story. He didn't have to read the story. The headline told him all he needed to know:

BLOUNT REPORTER, WIFE, CHILD
KILLED IN CRASH ON HIGHWAY

A: I sat there looking at the clipping and
       thought, I'm dead. I've already died.

T: Was it a shocking thought?

A: I'm not sure. I'm not sure of anything anymore. I think I was numb. The way I'm numb now.

T: Do you wish to suspend? It has been a grueling time for you. Important but grueling. A real breakthrough. But I think you should rest now. We can seek more details later.

A: Yes.

T: Let us suspend then.

END TAPE OZK012

I emerge from the drugstore and walk to the parking meter and my bike is gone. The five o'clock crowd passes by on the sidewalk, hurrying home from the office or the factory, feet scurrying over the pavement. A bus halts with a hissing and its doorway exhales people. Traffic lights flash on and off and car horns sound. And I stand there isolated by myself on a small invisible island, and I look at the spot where my bike had been. I shouldn't have left it there unguarded. I have my father's package in my hand and I hold it tightly, pressing it against my body, afraid that someone will rush by me and tear it from my grasp. I feel vulnerable, a headache beginning, a migraine maybe, a small spot of pain like a tumor throbbing in my forehead, above my eye. I touch the spot with my hand as if the pain is visible, touchable by my fingers. But mostly I stare dumbfounded at the spot where my bike had been.

I look around to see if someone has played a trick on me, a prank, has hidden the bike somewhere nearby. The mouth of an alley looms between two stores and I glance into the alley. Nothing but a few newspapers rolling in the wind, a rubbish barrel and a cat with arched back poised next to the barrel. The cat hisses and I turn away, glancing up and down the sidewalk. I encounter only strangers and no bike.

But the alley draws me again. If I had taken a bike, I'd have gotten out of there fast and the most likely route was the alley, a quick getaway, instead of the open exposure of the street where someone could yell "stop, thief."

I return to the alley. It's narrow, barely room for a boy and a bike to pass through, but I enter anyway, running through the narrow passage, my shoulders brushing the rough brick exterior. The alley is so narrow that claustrophobia threatens me again and my palms turn wet with perspiration while drops of sweat gather in my armpits. I plunge onward, through the alley, bursting finally out of it and find myself in a deserted area behind the Main Street buildings. Rubbish barrels; a derelict car, without wheels, sunk in the ground; boarded-up windows. Dusk hides whatever is in corners.

"Lose something, honey?"

I whirl around, surprised at the voice because there's no one or nothing there.

"Up here," the voice says, a faint southern accent softening the words.

He's standing on the fire-escape landing, above me on the second floor. Squinting, I see that he is huge, a mountainous man, with a white shirt open at the chest although it's cold in the New England dusk. As my eyes become accustomed to the twilight, I see that his face is moist, his plump cheeks wet, his forehead soaked. He has a handkerchief and he dabs ineffectually at his forehead. He leans against the iron railing of the fire escape and the railing creaks in protest. Instinctively, I back away a step or two, afraid that the entire structure will collapse, come crashing down. Had he called me "honey"?

"Somebody stole my bike," I say. "I left it in front of a store only for a minute or two and when I came out it was gone."

"That's right, honey, they'll steal anything these days. There used to be a saying, They'll steal anything that's not tied down, but these days they'll steal anything, even if it is tied down." The more he talks, the more pronounced his accent becomes.

I wonder if he can see my frown of distaste as I look at his monstrous body, all that sweat on a cold

evening, and the way his lips pronounce the word
honey. He repels me but I'm sure he knows something about the bike. Why had he asked whether
I'd lost something when he saw me standing there?

"Did you see anybody come running through
here with a bike?" I ask.

"You stay in one place long enough, you see a lot
of things," he says, his tone taunting now, as if he
wants to play a game. "Know what's hard? Being
this way, stuck in a cage this way, and having to
wait for everything to come to *you*, not being able
to go after anything. See what I mean?"

I see what he means. The iron railings and
banisters and rungs of the fire escape are cagelike
and he is a prisoner in his weight and his bulk.

"You live up there?" I ask, not wanting to play
games but not wanting to arouse his anger. He
wouldn't tell me anything if I turned him off too
fast.

"In an apartment here. Four rooms. I look out
the front windows at Main Street and I stand here
on the fire escape and look at the back alleys." He
gestures behind him, at a wide door, the kind of
door through which deliveries are made. "At least,
the place has a good-enough door. So I sit and wait
and look, or I stand and wait and look, and sooner
or later, I see something."

"I hope you saw my bike," I say, "and whoever
took it."

"Folks lose things, they sometime put an ad in
the paper. You know, saying: 'Lost, one bike, Main
Street of Hookset. Reward.' Reward, honey! That's

the key. You get something, you got to give a re-ward." His voice drips with a heavy southern ac-cent now and he pronounces "reward" as *ree-ward*. But there's more than a southern accent in his voice, something else lingers there but I don't want to recognize it.

"I'll give a reward," I say, almost imitating his accent. "I've got twenty-five dollars to give as a reward."

"There's all kinds of ree-wards, honey," he says. "There's ree-wards and ree-wards." And now, in the dusk, he begins to scratch at himself, scratching his chest where his shirt is open and where curly hair glistens. He scratches with both hands, de-scending to his stomach. "All kinds . . ." he says, his voice lingering in the twilight.

I am conscious again of the migraine, the throb in my forehead. A wave of nausea crests in my stom-ach and I taste acid and bile.

"All I want is my bike," I say, my lips trembling, and I'm sad and angry at the same time because I feel like a small boy again, still the coward I always was. There's a whimper in my voice and I hate my-self for the whimper and I hate the fat man up there on the fire escape for reducing me to this state. I also hate whoever took my bike and now I throb with more than a migraine's pain but with hate and anger. I stand helpless before him, shak-ing and trembling in the chill of evening, and I feel tears of helplessness and rage cold on my cheeks. His huge figure wavers in the wetness of my tears, as if he is somehow underwater.

"Aw, tell him who's got his bike," another voice intrudes, a sharp voice with the flint of New England in the words.

I wipe the tears away.

The fat man sighs a huge sigh that's like a wind able to topple trees.

"Go ahead, tell him." The voice comes from inside the apartment, behind the fat man.

The huge folds of flesh form a pout on the man's face. "Never can do what I want," he says, himself a little boy now.

"Tell him, Arthur," the voice says.

"The Varney boy—Junior—he took your bike," the man says. "Come through the alley there 'bout fifteen minutes ago. He's always stealing something, someday they're going to put him away."

"Where does he live?" I ask, sniffing, wondering how he can stand the cold.

"Upper Main Street next to the First Baptist Church. That's a joke—Junior Varney, biggest thief in town living next to a Baptist Church."

"You come in, Arthur, it's getting cold out there," the voice of the unseen man calls from inside, gently now, tenderly.

The big man looks down at me with a sadness in his eyes. Mournfully, he says, "I never get to do nothing."

"Thanks," I yell up, not at the big man but at whoever's inside. For some reason, I look at the massive man and find myself saying, "I'm sorry." I'm still sick to my stomach and my head throbs and I dread the prospect of tracking down Junior

Varney and I am still repelled at the lewdness of
the big man but he really looks caged as he turns
slowly away on the fire escape, so I say, "I'm sorry,"
again, and then I get the hell out of there.

TAPE OZK013   0800   date deleted T-A

T: You are looking well this morning.
A: Thank you.
T: You are alert.
A: I feel alert.
T: We are making excellent progress, are we not?
A: A lot of things are clearer now. Not everything. But enough. They give me the chills

sometimes but the chills are better than the blanks.

T: Good. I mentioned the necessity of specific details.

A: You're always talking about specifics—what kind of specifics?

T: I mean specific details as opposed to general information.

A: You mean, details of our lives in Monument and how we came to be there?

T: Yes, that, of course. Also, the why's of your presence in Monument.

A: But I've told you that. My father gave testimony. And this placed him in danger.

T: Did he ever tell you about his testimony, its nature?

A: No. There wasn't time.

T: What do you mean—there wasn't time? *(9-second interval.)*

A: I don't know. I'm not sure.

T: You appear troubled. You are frowning. Is anything the matter?

Like a cloud, hanging in the distance, in his mind, something dark lurking there. And the edge of panic again, a shiver in his bones, deep in his marrow . . .

T: Perhaps this line of questioning is disturbing you. Why not let the thoughts flow freely?

A: All right. It's just that, for a minute there,

I felt the blankness again. There are still blanks, you know.

T: And we shall fill those blanks eventually. Think of how far we have come to this point.

A: Do we still have a long way to go?

T: That depends.

A: You mean, it depends on me?

T: To a certain extent, yes. And on these sessions. And the medicine. Tell me, did you grow close to your father after you had discovered the truth of the situation?

A: Yes. We spent a lot of time together. He kept apologizing for the predicament he had placed me in, had placed my mother in, too. But I was proud of him, really. I mean, he had done what he believed to be right. He had given up his career . . .

He remembered asking his father, tentatively, afraid that he was invading his privacy, how much it had hurt him to start life over, to give up his old life, his career, his friends. Adam thought how terrible it would be if he had to leave Monument now, to give up Amy and start again in a new town, a new section of the country.

"Of course it hurt, Adam," his father said. "But it hurt your mother most of all. I didn't mind leaving Blount—I had always figured that my career lay elsewhere. I had those dreams a young guy has, dreams of going to distant places, fame, all that stuff. But your mother loved Blount, the people especially. The hardest thing for me—and I still miss it—was giving up newspaper work. I still hope that the situation will change and I'll be able to get back in the business someday. Grey figured it was too risky for me to continue in the same profession. Insurance didn't appeal to me. But the Department always keeps its eyes out for legitimate businesses they can buy or take over that one of their witnesses can operate. The insurance agency was available for me at the time. We had to build a new life, Adam. It was hard, naturally. But when you think of the alternative, we were glad to have a chance. There's always fear, though. Even today. Grey said our tracks are covered. Three bodies cremated ten years ago in Blount, New York. But who knows? Who really knows?"

"Why does Mr. Grey come here to Monument so often?"

"To keep in touch. He brings a special bonus of money twice a year. He also drops in to keep me up to date on developments. He also brings reassurances that we're still safe. Once in a while, he probes my memory for some lost fact, some overlooked detail that subsequent developments have made important. And there's another reason. He's never mentioned this reason—I only suspect it. I think he's keeping an eye on me."

"But why?"

"I don't really know. Maybe to see that I haven't been reached by the other side."

They were always on the move during these conversations, talking in snatches as they strolled the streets, visited the bazaar at St. Jude's Church, exchanging information as Adam aimed the ball at three wooden bottles arranged in a pyramid. Once they went to a drive-in movie and his father turned down the speaker while they conversed. A John Wayne film was on the screen—Adam had forgotten the title. But he remembered asking his father why all these precautions with Mr. Grey were necessary ten years after the testimony and threats.

Watching John Wayne swagger across the street, gun riding low on his hip, his father said, "Because nobody knows how powerful these organizations—maybe there's more than one—are today. Nobody knows how far they might have penetrated the government."

Adam was reluctant to use a certain word but he went ahead anyway, pulling his eyes away from John Wayne on the screen. "Does it involve the Mafia, Dad?" The word sounded ridiculous coming from him—melodramatic, belonging on a movie screen, maybe, but not in their lives.

"I can't say who or what, Adam. For your own protection. Anyway, the Mafia is only a handy word for people to use. There are a lot of words to describe the same thing. As far as time is concerned, the evidence I gave has been used and reused. But there's a catch. No one knows whether I divulged *all* the information, *everything* I knew. That's another reason for all this surveillance. And maybe it's the real reason for Grey's trips here. He keeps probing for more information and I tell him there isn't anymore, that I've held nothing back. And he just looks at me. That look gives me the chills. Sometimes, I think I'm an annoyance to him, an embarrassment. Sometimes, when he visits, we sit there like enemies. Or as if we're playing a crazy game that neither of us believes in anymore but the game has to go on . . .

T: This information your father talked about. Did he ever reveal its nature?

A: No.

T: Weren't you curious about it? After all, the information changed your lives.

A: He said he couldn't tell me, for my own protection, and I didn't press him for the information.

T: He said he told Grey that he was not holding back anything. Was he specific to you about that?

A: I don't know what you mean.

T: I mean, did you ever ask him whether he was telling Grey the truth or whether he was just being clever?
(*9-second interval.*)

T: Why this sudden silence? You are looking at me in a strange manner.

A: I think it's just the opposite. You're looking at me very strangely. It reminds me of what my father said about Mr. Grey. My father said the look on Mr. Grey's face gave him the chills. As if they were enemies. And that's the way you were looking at me a minute ago, that look on your face when you asked about the information—

T: I am sorry that you were disturbed by the expression on my face. I, too, am human. I have headaches, upset stomach at times. I slept badly last night. Perhaps that's what you saw reflected on my face.

A: It's good to find out you're human. Sometimes I doubt it.

T: I understand. It is just as well if you take out your anger on me. I don't mind.

A: I don't know what you're talking about.

T: Whenever we approach truths, basic truths that you've been trying to deny or hide, you turn upon me. But I understand. I am the only other target that's available.

A: What do you mean—the only other target? Who's the first target then?

T: Don't you know?

A: You mean—me? I get tired of all this—the way you twist things all the time.

T: You see? The anger again. Just as it happened when we were approaching an important area.

A: What area?

T: The information your father had, the information you say he didn't give you.
(*15-second interval.*)

Adam felt himself shriveling into the chair. Figuratively speaking, of course, because he knew that on the surface he was just sitting here as usual, looking at Brint. Brint, whom he was convinced now was

not a doctor at all. But then, who was he? Adam
recoiled from the possibilities. Was he an enemy?
One of those men who had been his father's enemy?
He felt the panic rising in him again and fought to
remain still, fought to ride out the panic as Brint
had always suggested. And he realized that he was
dependent on Brint. Whether he was an enemy or
not, Brint had helped him discover himself, who
he was, where he came from. Could he help him
discover what he was doing here? In this place? So
he knew he had to rely on Brint but he would be
careful, wary about the information Brint wanted.
And he thought, Was there really information
lodged within him that he didn't know about? Was
Brint, then, right, after all? His thoughts scurried,
like rats in a maze.

T: Are you ill?
A: No. I'm all right. All these discoveries.
       They keep throwing me off balance.
T: That is understandable.
A: The worst part is that my memories arrive
       piecemeal, in bits and pieces, the entire pic-
       ture isn't clear.
T: Let us take it all one step at a time.
A: Yes.
T: We were speaking of your father—how he
       was telling you about the past—let your
       mind wander in that direction—you and
       your father . . .

His father's explanations went on over a period of
weeks. Adam's questions were endless and the in-

formation he received sometimes made him shake his head in wonder and surprise. How you can be intimate with people, live with them twenty-four hours a day and not really know them. He was amazed at the deceptions that had been carried on by his parents through the years. Like his father's glasses—plain window glass brought to Monument by Mr. Grey, the style changing every two or three years. "That's why I avoid Dr. Huntley, the optometrist down the street from my office. I told him once that my closest friend is an optometrist in New York City—and that's where I got my glasses," his father explained.

His father's mustache also was part of the deception. He had not worn a mustache as a reporter in Blount. He had also given up cigarettes. "That was torture, Adam. But Grey insisted, and your mother was delighted to see me stop smoking. She said it was one of the few good things about our new lives. I'm still dying for a smoke today . . ."

Adam's questions seemed endless.

"Did you and Mom ever actually live in Rawlings, Pennsylvania?" Adam asked, telling his father of the visiting editor Amy had called him about.

"No. But we were flown there for a weekend visit so that we'd be acquainted with the town—the layout of the streets, the buildings, the feeling of the place—in case we ever encountered anyone from Rawlings. I remember standing outside the newspaper office there, thinking I'd like to meet the editor, talk shop. But I didn't. In fact, I've always avoided talking to Amy's father, afraid that I might betray myself." His father's voice was wistful.

What about his mother and those telephone calls to the woman who was Aunt Martha?

His father explained that Martha was a cloistered nun in a convent outside Portland, Maine. She was his mother's only living relative and Grey had allowed arrangements to be made for the weekly calls.

"It's the only risk Grey ever allowed, although it was a minimal risk," he said. "Your aunt had never lived in Blount and she had gone away to the convent as a teen-ager. A cloister is closed to the outside world, Adam. Never a visitor. Grey was able to arrange for a special dispensation to allow that weekly call—your mother's only link with the world she once knew . . ."

A: I am curious about something.
T: What is that?
A: You never ask about my mother. Only my father. As if you're not interested in her at all.
T: You are mistaken. It is you who doesn't speak of your mother. I have told you before—I am merely a guide. I do not lead you.
       (*15-second interval.*)
A: I want to talk about my mother. I mean, I want to find her in all these discoveries I'm making.

T: By all means. Go ahead.
       (10-second interval.)
T: What's the matter? Why the delay? Relax—
       take it easy.
       (5-second interval.)
A: Nothing—I can't even remember her face
       right now.
T: Take your time. She is there, a part of your
       life. She will come . . .

And she did, of course.

A: Funny about my mother. All my life, from the time I was just a little kid, I thought of her as a sad person. I mean, the way some people are tall or fat or skinny. My father always seemed the stronger one. As if he was a bright color and she was a faded color. I know it sounds crazy.

T: Not at all.

A: But later, when I learned the truth about our lives, I found she was still sad. But

strong, too. Not faded at all. It wasn't sadness so much as fear—the Never Knows.

T: What were these Never Knows?

A: Something she told me about one afternoon
when I got home from school . . .

That day, he found himself alone in the house with
his mother. She was sitting at the window, looking
out, a forlorn figure, wistful. He had not con-
fronted his mother like this ever since his discovery
of the past. She seemed to have been avoiding him,
refusing to meet his eyes, appearing very busy if he
approached. Once, he looked up at the dinner table
and saw his mother regarding him with tenderness—but a kind of terror in the tenderness—and
he wanted to go to her and fling his arms around
her. And he wasn't certain whether he wished to
bring reassurance to her or to himself.

This particular afternoon, she was caught off
guard when Adam came in the house. She turned
from the window and looked up at him, startled.

"You're early," she said.

"They called off the Lit. club meeting," Adam
responded. A lie—he hadn't felt like going to the
meeting.

"Let me make you some lunch," she said, getting
up, moving quickly as if she didn't want to be left
in the same room alone with him.

"Wait, Mom," he said, touching her arm.

She looked up at him, innocent, questioning.

"Let's talk, Mom," he said. "We haven't talked
in a long time."

"Oh, Adam," she said, tears gathering in her eyes, her face consumed with grief.

And he found himself holding his mother in his arms, trying to comfort her. She was suddenly the child, not Adam. And that was when she told him of her special terrors—the Never Knows.

"You see, Adam, it's never knowing what's going to happen, that's the worst thing. I've always been proud of your father and that decision he made back then. In many ways, it's been worse for him because he loved newspaper work so much and Mr. Grey said it would be too dangerous to continue in the work even with a new identity, a new name. So we came here, both of us, and tried to make the best of it. We even drilled ourselves. To be careful. To never use our real names, for instance. To be sure that you'd never suspect. I didn't mind the subterfuge. Actually, the things that really matter were still real to us. I've always been a Catholic and have gone to church and received the sacraments. I wanted you to be brought up Catholic, too. Mr. Grey arranged for papers to be made to show us as converts. So, you see, we kept our religion. And your father and I still had each other. And you. Mr. Grey kept telling us—and we had to agree—that the essential things had been kept, the things that mattered. We were a family together."

His mother was still looking out the window, as if watching for something. "And yet your father and I knew—we still know—that there are no guarantees. I sit here at the window and see a car come down the street and I wonder, Who's in that car, what do they want? And until the car passes by, I hold my breath. Even after the car has gone, I wonder, Were they studying the neighborhood, laying their plans . . .

"But who would they be, Mom?" Adam asked. "Weren't the people Dad testified against sent to jail? And how could they trace you?"

"That's the trouble, Adam. Maybe you become paranoid after a while, suspicious of everything and everyone, for no reason. But there are reasons, Adam. The people your father testified against are members of a huge organization, linked perhaps with other organizations. Like an evil growth: cut off one part and another part still grows. Your father's testimony killed one part, but who knows about the other parts? And then there's Grey, this Mr. Grey. Or Mr. Thompson or whatever he calls himself. He revealed to us once that he is identified in the government as a number—2222. He told us that when it was necessary for him to give us a way of reaching him in Washington in case of an emergency. We have placed our life in his hands, Adam. We have to trust him. In a way, he's our creator. He created the lives we lead today. He gave us names, decided what your father's profession would be. He also decided whether we could remain Catholic or not. I often wonder, Is it right to be at the complete mercy of this man, this number 2222? He's almost assumed the role of God in our lives, Adam. And this gives me the shivers."

She turned from the window. "Even now, we shouldn't be sitting here talking like this. The only safe place to talk, Grey says, is downstairs in the paneled room. Or outside, away from places that could be bugged. And here again, Adam, we're doing what Grey tells us. Sometimes I hate him. Fiercely. With a hate that's almost sinful. And I think, We trust him too much. What would happen if, for once, we defied him?" She shook her head ruefully. "We almost did, once or twice . . ."

"Tell me about it, Mom."

"One summer, we decided to take a vacation. The three of us. We would never leave you behind, of course. I've always wanted to go to New Orleans —the Mardi Gras, the jazz your father loves—such a colorful old city. But Grey ruled it out. He said New Orleans was off-limits that year."

"But why?" Adam asked.

"Because the people your father testified against have strong ties in New Orleans. We almost defied Grey. But we didn't, of course, because there was too much at stake. Another time, we wanted to go to Europe. But Grey said there would be too much fuss with passports. By fuss, he meant danger. So our hands were tied, Adam. That's what I mean about Grey—he rules our lives. And that's why I *do* defy him sometimes, in small ways. Talking like this, without going to the paneled room. And then I worry afterward because I think that I've exposed you and your father to danger. I don't care about myself anymore . . ."

Adam suddenly felt so sad, so sad.

"And always, Adam, there are the Never Knows. Never knowing who can be trusted. Never knowing

who that stranger in town might be. The phone
rings and I think, Is this the call I've always been
afraid of? Have we been discovered? A woman I've
never seen before glances at me in the supermarket.
And I worry. Because you never know. Even Grey.
I'm afraid to look at him sometimes. I avoid him,
in fact. Because we are at his mercy. He could snap
his fingers tomorrow and our lives could change
completely again."

Adam found himself afflicted with his own Never
Knows. He felt safe at home or at school but found
himself uneasy when he went downtown or walked
the streets. Instinctively, he kept an eye out for
strangers, people he had never seen before. He was
suddenly acutely conscious of the actions of other
people. Was that man heading in his direction?
Was someone following too closely behind him?
Did the man standing next to him at the newspaper
rack in Baker's Drugstore appear to be studying
him? Crazy, Adam told himself. I am the same person I have been for fourteen years. These are the
same people I have seen all these years. The only
difference was that Adam had never noticed them
before. Monument is a city of 33,000 people, he
told himself—he had done a study of the city for
his social science class at school—and he couldn't
expect to know everyone. Some faces had to be the
faces of strangers.

Suddenly, life became unbearably sweet to
Adam. Funny, he had taken the events of his life
for granted for a long time, the days and nights
passing routinely as if they'd continue forever, but

the threat to that life and the routines suddenly
made every minute and hour precious. Food had
never tasted so good before. He'd stop after school
to buy a Mister Goodbar or a Three Musketeers
and the candy was more delicious than it had ever
been. He also loved his father and mother more
and wanted to be with them. When they ate dinner
together, he felt a sense of intimacy with them, as
if he were more than just a son, more than someone
who was told to make his bed and take out the
rubbish. He was part of them. Somehow fear had
forged love.

T: So, it was not all nightmare then, was it?
A: No. There were good times when we were
       a family together. But sometimes I'd look in
       the mirror, studying myself, trying to find
       some remnants of my Italian heritage.
       Crazy—I'd joke about it—I didn't even like
       spaghetti. I'd look in the mirror and pro-
       nounce my name, the name I was born with.
       Paul Delmonte. But I'd only whisper it.
       Already I was abiding by my father's rules,
       by Mr. Grey's rules. Then there were times
       when I felt like standing on a rooftop and
       shouting to the world, "I am Paul Del-
       monte. I didn't die in that accident in New
       York." I'd think, Poor Paul. As if he had
       been another person and not me. My father
       said we had to live in the present, not the
       past. It was my mother who led me back to
       the past once.

T: Tell me about that time.

A: It was just a moment, just a glimpse . . .

During that period when he was learning about the past, Adam realized that despite her gentleness and wistfulness, his mother was more defiant than his father about their situation. His father played to perfection his role of insurance agent, Rotary Club member, Chamber of Commerce committeeman. Adam marveled at the performance, knowing that it was a performance. His father was always in character; Adam found it hard to believe he had been a crusading newspaperman. ("Well, not exactly crusading—investigative reporting is mostly monotonous work, digging through thousands of words for the one word that doesn't ring true.")

His mother was really the rebel. She often spoke resentfully, almost contemptuously, of Mr. Grey. "I sometimes think we were too unquestioning, Adam, too naive. Did your father really have to give up newspaper work? Weren't there any other alternatives?" Adam was delighted to see this defiance. He realized that his mother wasn't the compliant woman he had known before. Although she seldom smiled and sadness clung to her most of the time, she was capable of anger. And deception. One day, she studied Adam's face as if trying to make up her mind about something. Finally, she said, "Come with me, Adam."

She led him downstairs but not to the paneled room. There was a shadowy alcove at the other end of the cellar, filled with old furniture and other stuff. Adam recognized old wicker chairs they had used long ago in the summer, in the backyard. His mother waded through this debris of other years, clearing a path to a box tied with old rope, about four feet square, in the corner. Patiently, she untied the rope. She opened the box. Inside the box were blankets neatly folded, blue and white, patchwork quilts. His mother peeled off the blankets, like turning the pages of a book.

"Look," she said, holding up a jacket that seemed vaguely military. "Your father wore this in the army." Her probing uncovered a green scarf, soft, wispy, the material so flimsy that it seemed like fog. "Your father gave me this one Valentine's Day—he's always been so sentimental, your father." She held the scarf to her cheek, closed her eyes. "We had such a wonderful life, Adam—and when you came along, it seemed too good to be true. There are times when I think we had too much and we had to pay for it." His mother shivered slightly in the dampness of the cellar. She replaced the green scarf in the box and unfolded another blanket. "I suppose I should have thrown these things away a long time ago—they're relics of that other life and your father says that for the sake of safety, we have to forget that other life. And he's right, of course. But I cheated. I've kept a few things we had when we fled through the night. A pathetically few things— some of your baby things, an old hat your father used to wear . . .

"You're sentimental, too, Mom," Adam said, glancing into the box, wondering about those baby things of his. Not his, actually, but Paul Delmonte's.

The door bell rang upstairs, and his mother stiffened. So did Adam. The bell rang again.

"This is what I hate," his mother whispered, arranging the blankets in the box again, closing the cover. "This never-knowing. A door bell rings and it's like an alarm bell."

"I'll go up and see who it is," Adam volunteered, "while you tie up the box." And for the first time, Adam got a taste of what it was like for his mother, the deceptions that were a part of her life, and the constant threat of danger. Even if danger didn't exist, the possibility existed and this was maybe even worse. As it turned out, Amy was ringing the door bell.

"It's only Amy," Adam called out to his mother, wanting to reassure her that everything was all right.

"What do you mean—*only* Amy?" the girl asked, as Adam opened the door. "What kind of hello is that?"

He had been a stranger to Amy during this period. He met her briefly after school and walked home with her, but he made excuses for their not getting together, not carrying out more Numbers. She looked at him quizzically, obviously puzzled, but said nothing. He apologized for not accompanying her on the Number at the church parking lot. Actually, he had been relieved to have avoided the experience.

"That's okay," she had said. "I gave you a rain-check—we can pull it off at the next wedding."

One afternoon, as he left her on the corner near her house, she called to him, "Are you all right, Adam? You don't seem the same these days. Anything bugging you?"

Bugging. He thought of the paneled room downstairs. "No, Amy," he said. "It's my mother. She's not feeling well and I try to spend more time at home."

Actually, he was in agony. He desperately wanted to share his predicament with Amy—he wanted to share his entire life with her—but his father had sworn him to secrecy. It's life and death, Adam, his father had said.

Life and death . . .

T: There is panic in your eyes again. Did those words—life and death—disturb you?

A: I don't know. Every once in a while, a dark cloud, something like a dark cloud, crosses my mind.

T: Do specific words or specific thoughts bring the black cloud?

A: Sometimes. But the blankness always brings it. Not always, really. I can stand the blanks sometime. But other times, there's terror in the blanks.

T: At this very moment, for instance?

A: Yes. I wonder, What happens next? Or, rather, what happened back then? And I

don't know. I don't know. Then the terror
comes. Yes, that's when the terror comes.
(10-second interval.)

T: You must relax. You must not become agi-
tated. Perhaps a pill. To calm you down.
This is merely an anxiety attack. This gasp-
ing for breath—this is only anxiety. Try to
relax.
(5-second interval.)

A: What happened back then? What happened?
(10-second interval.)

A: Where's my father? Where's my mother?

T: You must calm yourself.

A: What's happened to them? Where are they?

T: Please, you must control yourself.

A: What's happening? What's happening to me
now? What's going on? I feel—

T: I think medication is necessary. I have rung
and they are coming. The medicine will
calm you, take away the terror.

A: What's going on? What's happening?

T: Let us suspend for now. I think it is best.
They are arriving—

A: Please—

T: Suspend.

END TAPE OZK013

———————

I am a spy. I am across the street from the Varney House on Upper Main Street in Hookset, Vermont, and it is dark now and cold and my cap is pulled down over my ears and my hands are stiff with chill as I clutch my father's package. My body is pressed against a stone wall that divides a Salvation Army building from an abandoned supermarket. Upper Main Street is quiet and the rush hour is over. Occasionally, people pass by the sidewalk, and I can almost reach out and touch their elbows but they don't see me. I look across the street and I can see the bike. Or, at least, I can see the handlebars where they stick up above the banister of the front porch. The bike is so near and yet so far. It would be so easy to run up the front walk and grab the bike and then pedal away. But there are always people coming and going into the house. The Varney family is a big family with people of all ages going in and out of the house, as if it's some kind of boardinghouse. So I wait for the evening to quiet down, for the comings and goings to halt.

At least my headache is gone. I had stopped at a drugstore and bought a small tin of aspirin and then asked the clerk at the soda fountain to pour me a glass of water. I gulped three aspirins and then threw the rest of them in a trash container. I didn't want to be found with pills on me; how could anyone be sure they were aspirins—so many pills look alike. I think again of the capsules that I didn't take this morning but now I'm glad I didn't take them. I have survived the terrible moments of being without them and my head is clear and my senses alert and I need all the sharpness I can muster to get the bike back. I have to move fast, no wasted motion, and I can't afford to stumble or hesitate.

I could have gone to the police, of course. But I didn't want to take any risks. I am so near Rutterburg now. Belton Falls and the motel is only a mile or two away and I can easily make it to Rutterburg in the morning and I don't want to take a chance of

the police asking questions and wondering what
someone from Massachusetts is doing in the dark of
night up in Vermont. All I want is to get my bike
back and then find the motel and sleep, rest my
weary bones and aching legs and then pedal into
Rutterburg, Vermont, tomorrow morning in the
sunshine.

The front door of the Varney house slams and I
am alert again, holding my breath, tensing my
body. A boy of about my own age comes out of the
house and stands there for a moment, looking
around, looking up and down the street, as if he
senses he is being watched. I shrink and shrivel
against the stone wall. He walks to the bike and
runs his hands over the handlebar as if he is cares-
sing it. While he's inspecting the bike, a woman
comes out of the house and approaches him. They
talk a while and I can't hear them. The woman
places her hand on the boy's shoulder and he
wrenches away from her.

Suddenly, I miss my mother. I want to cry. I
want to feel her hand on my shoulder. I watch the
woman standing near the boy. She's still talking
and he doesn't look at her, his back to her. I hate
him. Not only for stealing my bike but for turning
his back on his mother. He has a mother and he
turns his back on her. I feel like dashing across the
street to attack him, knock him down, feel the frac-
ture of bone as my fist hits his jaw. But I stay there,
breathing hard, waiting my chance, not wanting to
think of my mother, holding off the anguish, the
loneliness. Then the woman goes into the house

and the boy stands there for a moment more. Then
he takes the bike and wheels it to the steps, guides
it down the three steps from the porch to the front
walk, and begins to wheel it across the lawn. He
turns the corner and is heading toward the back of
the house.

That's when I make my move. I can't afford to
let him out of my sight or allow him to disappear
into the backyard because the yard is an unknown
quantity and I don't know the conditions there. So,
I yell, "Hey, Junior Varney," mustering all my
vocal strength, and at the same time I run across
the street, a passing car brushing me slightly as I
burst into the roadway.

Junior Varney stops, dumbfounded. He draws
the bike close to him as if it's a shield. My heart
pounds furiously as I approach him. In dismay, I
see that he is taller and heavier than I am. I sigh,
sadly. It's never easy, never easy.

"That's my bike," I say.

"What are you talking about?" he answers, bel-
ligerently. He is prepared to fight and I feel like
crying again.

"The bike. It's mine. You stole it on Main
Street."

"You're crazy," he says. "I bought this bike from
a kid this afternoon. I paid him fifty bucks for it."

"You're lying."

"*You're* the liar. You're the goddam liar. You
better get out of here or you'll get massacred."

I am terrified but I reach out and grab the handlebars. I drop my father's package and wrench at

the bike. This is my bike and I am riding it into Rutterburg, Vermont, tomorrow morning and nothing is going to stop me. Nothing. I pull at the bike and Junior Varney and I are caught in a ridiculous tug-of-war and the air is filled with our breathing, no other sound, as if we are alone on the planet. Finally, he pushes against me and I lose my balance and fall. I hit the ground and roll over. He tries to run, holding onto the handlebars. I dive at him. I grab his feet. He trips, pitches forward, and lets go of the bike as he falls. He hits the pavement, his crunch sickening as he strikes the concrete. In that brief interval between the time he feels the impact and begins to gather himself together, I take possession of the bike. It is mine. I swivel it around. I bend down and pick up the package. As he manages to get to his knees, I am running with the bike toward the street. I glance back and see him staggering to his feet, rubbing his jaw in a daze, and I am on the bike now, sailing, sailing, down the street, on the wrong side of the street and with no lights on the bike, but I am going, going—I have the bike back, I am pedaling beautifully and I am on my way again to Rutterburg.

TAPE OZK014   2155   date deleted T-A

T: You summoned me. You wish to talk?
A: Yes—I don't know. I know it's late but I
        couldn't sleep. I slept earlier. They gave me
        a shot. But I woke up and couldn't sleep
        again and I didn't want another shot.
T: I am pleased that you wanted to speak to me.
A: I don't know whether I do or not.
T: Is it a question of trust again?

A: Yes. I guess that's it.

T: Why this distrust on your part?

A: Because I don't know anything about you. You say your name is Brint but that's all you've told me. I don't know whether you're a doctor or not. There is a doctor here—he gives me the shots, the medicine—he's kind.

T: What has convinced you that he is a doctor and I'm not? Simply because he wears a white coat and I prefer a business suit? Because he administers medication and I don't? Because he has a soothing bedside manner, which I obviously lack?

A: More than that.

T: What then?

A: I thought at first that you were a psychiatrist, leading me to the past, to find out all about myself.

T: Haven't I done that?
   (10-second interval.)

A: Yes.

T: Then why the doubt, why this constant distrust?

A: Because you always direct me along certain paths.

T: But isn't that part of my function? How many times must I reiterate that I am merely your guide to the past. I don't direct you. In fact, I often follow where you lead.

A: But it's as if you're searching for certain information—these specifics you're always talking about—and this information seems to be more important than anything else about me.

T: Poor boy. Consider this: how far we have come. From those first meager clues, the bus and the dog, to the vast amount of knowledge we have uncovered about yourself.

A: I know. And I'm grateful for what I've learned but—

T: But what?

A: It's still incomplete. The blanks are still there. In fact, sometimes I'm a blank. I find myself here talking to you and don't remember where I came from, whether from my room in this place or someplace else altogether. And sometimes it seems we have been through all this before, that the questions are the same questions I've heard a thousand times before.

T: There is a necessary amount of repetition. There are times when you are responsive and times when you are not.
   (*15-second interval.*)

A: I'm tired. My mind is tired.

T: Do you wish to return to your room?

A: No. That's the funny thing. At least here, I know I exist.

T: Let us talk awhile then. About things that don't distress you. Pleasant things.

A: Without looking for information?

T: Without looking for information.

A: Amy. I think of Amy a lot.

T: Are the thoughts of Amy happy thoughts?
A: Most of the time. Those Numbers of hers—
        sometimes they are so clear to me—she is so
        clear to me. Then the thoughts get lost.
T: Let your thoughts drift to Amy. Those
        Numbers. The good times. You say you love
        her. Did you ever share the knowledge of
        your life with her?
A: No. But—

But how he had wanted to. During those first turbulent days when he was learning about the past and their present situation from his parents, Adam realized, almost guiltily, that a kind of adventure had taken hold of his life. He felt set apart from the other kids at school—but not the loneliness of isolation his shyness had sometimes brought him. It was a different kind of aloneness, something exclusive, almost sweet. The agony of it all was the secrecy, knowing that he was pledged forever to tell no one—not even Amy. And this was the part that hurt, of course. He wanted to say to her: "We —my mother and father and me—are living through a Number that's the biggest one of all." One of the reasons why he avoided Amy in that period is that he was afraid he would tell her everything, that the secret would come tumbling out of him. He was afraid that he would be unable to resist dramatizing himself to her—"Look, Amy, I'm not just shy and awkward Adam Farmer, but a fugitive on the run, leading a double life. I am Paul Delmonte."

So he avoided her, didn't call her up, pretended he was busy or that his mother was ill. Thus, there also was a sadness in him in those days, a quiet sorrow deep within him that he did not allow to come to the surface.

"I'm sorry about all this," his father said once, apparently sensing the sadness.

And Adam had not told him about Amy and his longing for her and the most dangerous longing of all—that he might brag to her of what had happened to make himself more attractive to her, to make him a kind of hero in her eyes.

T: And did you ever tell Amy Hertz anything? Anything at all?

A: Nothing. Never. Even that day—

T: What day?

The day the phone call came. The day his mother said she dreaded: a call that could change their lives again. Adam learned about the call when he arrived home late on a Saturday morning from the Number he and Amy Hertz had finally pulled in the church parking lot. But the Number had fizzled.

"Sorry, Ace," Amy had said. "This is not one of my glorious moments."

The concept was fine but the execution misfired, something that was beyond Amy's control. They had lingered at the edges of the parking lot while the cars arrived sporadically during the half hour before the wedding was scheduled to begin. It was a ten o'clock wedding. He had felt sentimental watching the people arrive, everybody dressed up, families together, fathers and mothers holding the hands of small children as they made their way to the church.

As if reading his mind, Amy said, "Isn't that nice, Adam? I think it would be nice to be married someday and have kids running all over the house." She seldom called him Adam, only at tender moments.

He reached out and touched her hand, fumbling for it for a moment, and then held onto it. She smiled at him. He wanted to say, "I love you, Amy." But couldn't. She'd probably laugh and make a wisecrack and call him "Ace" again. He felt depressed suddenly. Would his secret keep him forever apart from other people, create a chasm between them? Could he never be intimate with anyone else again?

"So what's the Number, Amy?" he said, the words coming out of his confusion and sadness.

"Well, okay," she said reluctantly. She always withheld information about the Numbers until the last possible moment, stretching out the drama. "I am a sucker for drama," she always said.

"Look, Ace, there's going to be about a hundred cars in the lot when the wedding starts inside. And you'll notice most of them aren't locked. I don't know—there's something about a church parking lot that makes people feel safe. Anyway, after everybody's inside, we go to work."

"And how do we go to work?" Adam asked. It was a beautiful morning, the wind kicking at the small blades of grass, the sun dancing on the car hoods and windshields as the cars drove into the lot.

"Simple. We each take half the cars in the lot, sneak into them—everybody's in the church watching the bride so we don't have to worry too much about that—and then we do two things. First, we snap on the radio and turn the volume to high. Second, we turn the windshield wiper to the 'On' position. And then we get out of the car and go to another one."

"I don't get it," Adam said. "The motors are off—the radios won't play and the windshield wipers won't work."

"That's exactly right," she said, voice patient. "Nothing will work until the drivers get into their cars—about a hundred of them—and start the motors. Then the radios will explode like mad in their ears and the windshield wipers will go into action. Can you imagine all of them sitting there, wondering what in the world happened?"

"Yeah," Adam said. He could see it—but somehow he couldn't get excited about it. First of all, he wasn't crazy about getting into people's cars. That sounded like trouble if you were caught. Second, he didn't know how much impact a radio and windshield wipers would have on the people in the car. He looked at Amy, the excitement in her eyes, and he didn't want to disappoint her. But he was disappointing himself really. He thought, Am I outgrowing the Numbers? Has so much happened in my own life that I'm leaving them behind?

"What's the matter, Ace?" Amy asked, troubled suddenly.

For one desperate moment, he wanted to confess everything to her, but he knew that it was impossible.

"Nothing," he said.

And Amy, who had become accustomed to his moods, didn't press the matter further. After a while, she said, "Let's go." And they stole like movie Indians into the lot, attacking the cars, twisting the dials—until sudden shouts broke his concentration as he searched for the wiper button that seemed to be completely hidden in an old Buick convertible.

He looked up and saw a man running out of the church toward the lot. He wore an old corduroy jacket; he certainly wasn't a member of the wedding party. Probably the church janitor.

Adam froze, stunned, thinking, I can't risk exposure. Amy's voice reached him from nearby: "Run, Ace, run. They saw us." Adam grappled with the door handle, turned it. He heard the sound of running feet and took a quick glance backward. The man was weaving in and out of the cars, like a drunken basketball player, yelling at Amy to stop, to halt, to come back here this minute . . .

Amy was a blur as she ran across the lot toward a clump of trees. No one would ever catch Amy. Adam also realized that the man had not seen him at all. After the man had passed by, Adam made his way as casually as possible to the front of the lot and started walking down the street, remembering Amy's advice: "Act nonchalant, always act as though you belong wherever you are." He thought of the way she had scooted through the lot but having warned him first. That Amy. How he loved her.

They met, by prearrangement (Amy delighted in all these strategies) at Baker's Drugstore; that was their assembly spot, both before and after all the Numbers.

"Sorry, Ace," she said. She'd arrived ahead of him and was already sipping an ice-cream soda. Chocolate with vanilla ice cream, as usual. "How many cars did you do?" she asked. "I only did about five before the guy spotted me. He yelled, 'Stop thief,' just like in the movies. It was kind of funny in a way . . ."

And then for some reason they got the giggles and laughed a lot, annoying Henry Sanett, the clerk who was about sixty and couldn't stand anybody under forty, and Adam drank two vanilla milkshakes and they talked about other Numbers, the A&P, and it was nice there in the store, on a sunny windswept day, Amy across from him in the booth, flushed, lovely. The thought crossed his mind, She's my girl, isn't she? My girl.

Later they parted, Adam to go home for lunch, although his stomach bulged with the milkshakes, and Amy to meet her father at the newspaper. "Call me," she said over her shoulder as she walked away.

Adam walked home, kicking at sidewalk debris, thinking of Amy—car radios and windshield wipers, for cripes sake—and arrived to find that the nightmare had already started. Without him.

His mother was at the door, her face the color of fog, her eyes like shattered marbles.

"What's wrong?" he asked.

"Grey called," his mother said. "An emergency."

T: Ah, you see why you need me? Why these sessions are so important?

A: Why?

T: The discoveries, even when you are not searching. You came here tonight because you were restless and you said you did not trust me and you began to speak freely, of Amy, and in the process we uncover more information—this emergency—
(5-second interval.)

A: Maybe I don't want to uncover it. I feel nauseous. I'm tired.

T: I don't think you have any choice in the matter.

A: What do you mean?

T: I think you have reached the point where you cannot stifle the memories, whatever you wish to call them, any longer. In fact, this is what drew you here to this room, tonight, this need to remember. The memories are there—they must come out, they must emerge, they cannot be allowed to fester any longer.
(8-second interval.)

T: It is not a matter of trust any longer, it

> is a matter of inevitability. The knowledge
> must come, you cannot hold it back.

A: I know, I know . . .

And he did know. He knew the knowledge was
there waiting to come forward, welling up inside
him, waiting for him to express it, verbalize it, and
in that way make it real. But at the same time, he
hesitated. A part of himself resisted.

T: What is the matter?
A: Let me wait a moment.
T: The time is past for waiting.

He knew that but he also knew that Brint, or
whoever he was, was sitting across from him, waiting, like a predator, an enemy—he was certain of
that now—but he knew also that he had to reveal
everything to him, that he could not do it alone.

All he could hope for was that he could find the
knowledge about himself without betraying—betraying who?

T: Tell me—tell me about this emergency
        with Grey.
A: Yes. I'll tell you . . .

He could tell that his mother was upset, the way
her hands trembled slightly as she drew him into
the living room. And yet he was impressed by the
calmness of her voice, the crispness of her words.
She was upset, all right, but in control.

"Everything's going to be all right," she said, her voice firm, as if she were commanding it to be firm. Adam thought of all the times parents assure their children that everything was fine when everything wasn't fine but they had to play the role for the sake of the children.

"Where's Dad?" Adam asked.

"Down at the office, taking care of a few details. We have to go away for a few days, Adam."

"Where are we going? And why? What's it all about?" he asked, hearing his voice rising, wishing he could be in control the way his mother was.

She took his hands and drew him into the living room. "This has happened once in a while, Adam. It's like a fire drill at school. Or maybe a bomb scare. Anyway, Grey called an hour or so ago. He thinks that our identities may be known. He isn't sure, chances are he's mistaken, but he insists that precautions be taken."

"But how does he know?"

She blew air out of her mouth, impatiently. "This is the ridiculous part of it all, Adam. Remember, I told you about the Never Knows and how you always had to play it safe? Well, Grey has his Never Knows, too. He said one of his men overheard a conversation on a wiretap in which Monument was mentioned—"

"A wiretap?" But this is absurd, Adam thought, this has nothing to do with me and Amy Hertz and the Numbers and school and my father and mother.

"Yes. The Department has to keep a check on certain people. And Monument was mentioned in a conversation. A date was also mentioned. Tomorrow. Now, it could be nothing. In fact, the Monument that was being referred to might not even be us, this city. Probably it's a real monument. But Grey thought that no chances should be taken. He suggested that we leave for a few days, take a trip, a vacation. Meanwhile, his men will be in town, watching the house, checking out any suspicious developments."

"You said this kind of thing had happened before?" Adam asked.

"Yes. Twice, actually. The first time was one of those strange coincidences. The town observed its two hundredth anniversary a few years ago—it was one of the first towns to be settled in this area. We had parades and a lot of activities, just like the country's bicentennial. Television crews came from all over—Boston, Worcester, even New York—to film the events. One television network planned a special program on how a small town celebrates a bicentennial—they sent TV people here for a week or two, to conduct interviews and film people and places. Grey thought it might be wise if we went away for those two weeks—the government paid for a vacation in Maine. Two weeks of coast and beaches. But somehow it was hard to enjoy it all—knowing why we were there."

"I think I remember that trip," Adam said. "I remember that I was kind of disappointed. I was going to march in the big parade with the Boy Scouts and suddenly we were heading toward Maine and you and Dad kept saying what a great time we were going to have but it sounded as if you were apologizing."

His mother nodded. "All the guilts your father and I have piled up, Adam," his mother said, the sadness in her voice again.

"What was the other time?"

"A scare like this. A witness before a congressional committee in Washington said that he had secret knowledge of a former newspaperman who had given earlier evidence. He said the newspaperman had vanished under mysterious circumstances but was now an agent in the Northeast. This was all very vague, of course, but Grey felt that we should not take any chances. Again, we went on another vacation. This time to California. San Francisco. For a week. And it rained every day and you had a cold and a fever. You were only seven years old. Then it turned out that the witness had not been referring to your father at all but to another newspaperman who had turned out to be an agent for the CIA."

The door bell rang. The tension again; his mother suddenly stiff like in a movie freeze frame. The key turned in the door and his father stepped into the hallway.

"Good, Adam," he said. "You're home." He looked at Adam's mother. "You've told him?"

For the first time, Adam noticed crevices of age on his father's face, small chasms of hidden depths.

His father advanced briskly into the living room. "Look," he said, "I think we can use a weekend away from Monument. Probably drive north—it's beautiful this time of year up there. We'll find a nice motel and maybe an old inn and have ourselves an old-fashioned New England dinner." He clapped his hands a couple of times as if in anticipation of the trip ahead, as if it were really a pleasure trip. "I think we can all use a change of scene—I know I can. And, Adam, we can call the school from on the road Monday and tell them you're taking the day off. That'll give us the rest of today, Sunday and Monday. And, who knows, maybe we'll take Tuesday, too."

His father's voice was buoyant, eager—and Adam suddenly realized, with a chill, the truth: his father was playing the game, not trusting the walls, acting as if no phone call had been received from Mr. Grey. His face was still haggard and his eyes wary and haunted and the bright enthusiastic voice was a sharp contrast.

"Well, shall we pack?" he said, turning to Adam's mother.

She smiled, wanly. "I've already packed. I always keep the suitcases ready."

His father walked over to Adam and put his arm around his shoulder. "It's going to be all right, Adam," he whispered. Actually whispered—here in their own living room. What have they turned us into? Adam thought. What has Mr. Grey done to my father and mother to make this kind of thing possible? For the first time, the horror of their predicament became real to Adam.

"Let's go," his father said, his hand clutching Adam's shoulder, a deep sadness in his eyes.

"Okay, Dad," Adam said.

His mother had already gone upstairs for the suitcases.

> (*20-second interval.*)
> T: Do you wish to rest awhile?
> A: No. I want to get through it all. Finally. My head hurts and I don't want a pill. I want to end it, get to the end—
> T: Let us proceed then . . .

TAPE CHANGE:
END OZK014

The motel is on the outskirts of Belton Falls and I pedal toward the place. It's dark now and I know it is dangerous being on the road without lights or reflectors and wearing a khaki jacket but I am in a hurry and don't want to walk. Every bone in my body seethes with pain and weariness and my lungs burn and my hands and feet are freezing, but I go on pedaling. The cars sweep by, the headlights blinding me sometimes, and once in a while a horn blows at me and the sound wails in the darkness, but I keep going. It's only a half mile or so out of the town across from a gasoline station, that's where the motel is. And now I remember its name: Rest-A-While Motel, and it has cabins and my mother said, "Isn't this romantic?" and we stayed there. Most of the cabins were for two people but they moved a cot in for me so that we could be together all night long. And I lay there in the cot and felt safe and secure, listening to my father snore and hearing my mother breathe, the way her breath fluttered a bit as if a butterfly danced on her lips.

So I dig in and pedal, past the stores and the houses, and a long warehouse that I pass as if it's a big silent ship, and a motorcycle roars past me and almost blasts me from the road. Then, finally, I see the lights of the gas station across from the motel and my heart leaps and I yell, "Hooray." I have made it to the motel. I have come this far and nothing has stopped me, nothing will stop me now. I will sleep tonight in the cabin where I stayed last year with my mother and father and I will be secure and safe again, thinking of them. And then tomorrow I will wake up and arrive in Rutterburg, Vermont, across the river.

The motel is dark. The light above the sign isn't lit and the sign swings eerily in the wind. The cabins have an abandoned look. Is the place closed for the season, like the ice-cream stands along the way? I check the cabin that serves as the office and it, too, is deserted. I park my bike and walk up to the office. The door is swinging slightly, unlocked.

I push it open and the smell of staleness fills my nostrils, the odor of something old and passed by. The streetlights throw a pale illumination into the office. Two chairs are piled on one another in a kind of obscene embrace. The desk is cluttered with papers and books and other debris as if someone abandoned it hurriedly. I wonder what time it is and where I can find another place to stay tonight. My head throbs and my body longs for rest. I won't need any medicine to sleep tonight.

I take the two chairs apart and sit in one of them, resting for a moment. I am so weary. It is amazing to me how much the place has changed since last year—the cabin seems or rather *feels* as if it has been neglected for years and years. I think of how fast decay moves in and it makes me shiver. I think of my pills and wish for the thousandth time I had taken them along. I think of the stories of drug addicts who break into stores and murder other people to get their fixes and I can understand them. Right at this minute, I would give anything to be folded into bed, the pills working their magic, soothing me.

A sound breaks the silence. Somebody is outside, near the bike. I leap to my feet and stalk to the doorway, my legs protesting.

A dog is poking his nose at the front wheel of the bike. A small dog, a cocker spaniel, frisky and energetic. I am not afraid of cocker spaniels and I chase it away. "Go on, go on, get out of here," I say. The dog studies me for a moment and then lopes away, tail wagging.

The service-station attendant across the street is pumping gas into a car. He's a teen-ager with long dark hair flowing to his shoulders. I would like to be like him: to have a job and perform it well and collect my pay at the end of the week and go out with a girl, like Amy. I envy him and I don't even know him. I think about the friends he must have and his family. I feel alone. "Okay," I tell myself, "cut the crap, stop the self-pity. This gets you nowhere."

The wind comes up and I shiver again, turning away from the service station across the street. The wind bangs the door to the office and I see what I must do: get something to eat and then return here and sleep. I can curl up on the floor and prop a chair against the door, against the doorknob for protection, and sleep the night away. And then tomorrow, fresh and rested, I can make the last few miles to Rutterberg and get there in triumph, flying fast on the bike. Now I'll get something to eat and call up Amy Hertz and tell her my mission is almost accomplished and then come back and sleep sweetly through the night. And then I have an even better idea: Why sleep in the cabin's office? Why not investigate the other cabins? Maybe they've left beds and mattresses and blankets there. I guide my bike to the first cabin and look in the window. The window is dirty, fly-specked, spotted. I squint and see a bed, the mattress naked and askew. What the hell, as Amy would say, a mattress is better than a floor.

I walk across the street. The attendant is checking the oil in a car, probing around with the dip-stick.

"Have you got a pay phone?" I ask.

His long hair swirls as he lifts his head and looks at me. "No booth," he says. "Just a phone on the wall." He looks at me and my bike without interest; I don't represent potential profit for him.

I walk across the grease-spotted pavement and enter the office. The smell of oil fills the air. And old rubber. I see a vending machine with candy bars and figure that I will stock up for the evening. I read somewhere that chocolate gives you quick energy.

The phone clings to the wall near the door that leads to the garage itself. I scoop out my change once more and insert the dime and wait for the operator. A man's voice says: "Operator . . ."

I pronounce the numbers carefully, exaggerating them, almost a burlesque, but I don't care, I don't want to risk another wrong number. The lights of passing cars flash by, and I realize that I could never have made it this far tonight alone, on the bike.

The phone is ringing, ringing.

I lose count of the rings.

And then: "Hello, hello." That same gruff, impatient voice, not Amy's father, not anybody I know.

"Hello," I say. "Is Amy there?" I feel ridiculous asking the question because I know it's futile.

A pause and then as if he's being very patient:

"There's nobody named Amy here. You the kid called earlier? I'm telling you, there's no Amy here."

It's cold suddenly in the office.

"Look, mister, there must be some kind of mistake. Is this Monument, Massachusetts, 537–3331?" Again I pronounce the numbers carefully, enunciating with precision.

"Yes, this is Monument, Massachusetts, 537–3331," he says, sarcastically, mimicking my voice.

My hand trembles as it holds the phone. The office is getting colder, as if someone had just opened a door and allowed in the coldest air in the world.

"Then there must be some mistake," I say. Is it possible for the telephone company to goof that badly—issue the same number to two different places in town?

"Yeah, I guess there is," the man says. "Look, kid, I been holed up in bed with some kind of flu and I don't appreciate being dragged to the phone like this—"

"Mister, I'm sorry to bother you. But 537–3331 is a right number. It's the number of a family by the name of Hertz. And I've been calling it for the past six months. I called it yesterday, for crying out loud."

The cold has invaded my body now, seeped into my bones, a cold like no other I have ever felt, penetrating, relentless.

"Look, kid, the phone company doesn't make

that kind of mistake. This is Monument, Massachusetts, and my number is 537–3331—I've had it for three years—and I don't know any Hertz family."

I am trembling all over now. I should have taken the medicine this morning. I shouldn't have thrown it away.

I manage to say, "Thank you."

Before he hangs up, he says, "Try Directory Assistance. Just don't ring this number anymore."

I see the phone book dangling from a chain.

I open it. I find the number for Directory Assistance.

My hands shake but I find another dime and put it in the slot.

I have never been so cold in all my life but it's a cold coming from inside. I dial the numbers. One. And the area code: 617. And the rest of it: 555–1212.

"Directory Assistance—what city?" The voice is like a sound from a machine.

"Monument," I say. I tell her the name—Hertz —and address and I wait and I am surprised that my hand is so steady holding the phone when the rest of my body is trembling.

"Hertz," she says. "There's a Hertz Rent-A-Car on Main Street—but no other Hertz in Monument. Was that the right spelling—H-e-r-t-z?"

"Thank you," I say and hang up.

And I watch my hand replacing the receiver and it's as if I am caught in some kind of slow-motion film. The man had said 537–3331 had been his number for three years. Three years. I turn away

from the telephone and begin to move and I find
that it's hard to place one foot in front of the other.

The attendant turns his head as I approach. He is
wiping the windshield. There's a woman in the car.
Her face is distorted by the liquid that's been
sprayed on the windshield.

"Yeah?" the attendant asks, but not really interested. He is chewing gum and his jaw moves
languidly. Who has slowed up everything? The
world is in slow motion.

"How long's the motel across the street been
closed?" I ask, trying to hurry the words, but it's
hard to talk in slow motion.

He looks at me funny. Strange, I mean.

And the woman's face is still distorted as she
squints through the windshield.

I look across the street at the cabins and the
attendant also looks.

"Oh, hell, two or three years, I guess. At least."

He begins to wipe the windshield again.

I touch his shoulder. It's an effort to raise my
hand to his shoulder but I do it, anyway, slowly and
carefully.

"The cabins weren't open last summer?" I ask,
saying the words carefully, not wanting to say the
wrong words.

He stops wiping the windshield now and stares
at me. I don't like the stare. There's something
strange in the stare, as if I am alien, a visitor from
another planet, another galaxy. The woman pokes
her head out the window. Her hair is gray but she

has Orphan Annie eyes, wide, no lashes; she looks as if she has never blinked in her life.

"You all right?" the attendant asks. And his eyes are wide, too. His words don't seem synchronized with his mouth, as if a soundtrack has gone askew.

Why didn't I take the pills this morning?

Clutching the package with one hand and pushing the bike with the other, I start across the street. I can feel the attendant and the woman staring at me, their stares piercing the back of my head, but I don't turn back. A terrible sound fills my ears, like a cry of doom. My teeth suddenly hurt; my mouth is open and the cold air bruises my teeth, causing them to ache. I try to close my mouth but can't do it; it's as if my jaw is locked, never to be closed again. And then I realize that the sound I hear is me. I am screaming and I can't stop. The sound is terrible. A car brushes past me, then another: flash of lights, blare of horn.

"Hey, watch where you're going," someone calls.

Finally, I am across the street, the bike, the package, and me. The grass is soft beneath my feet and I think I have stopped screaming now because everything is quiet. I check my mouth and it's still open but I am not screaming any longer. I push toward the cabin where my mother and father and I stayed, all together, nice that night, the three of us together. I place the bike carefully against the cabin. I look across the street at the gas station and the attendant is standing there looking at me. The Orphan Annie woman is out of the car now and also looking. My mouth is still open and maybe I'm still screaming.

I turn away, and beat at the cabin door asking them to let me in, to please let me in . . .

The darkness gathers me.

TAPE CHANGE:

START:
TAPE OZK015   2218   date deleted T-A

A: It was like an adventure in the beginning,
         the three of us going off in the car. . . .

Although the day was dark and overcast, one of
those muted October days when autumn's brilliant

colors are suddenly subdued, Adam felt exhilaration as his father drove the car north, out of Monument into Fairfield and across the New Hampshire line into Carver.

They all sat in the front seat, a bit cramped, his mother in the middle, and this was the only disturbing note. "I think it might be better if we sit together," his father had said. And Adam felt a small shiver—were things so bad that it was dangerous for one of them to sit alone in the back seat?

It began to rain at one point but this did not dampen their spirits. The windshield wipers swung on the glass like a metronone and Adam said, "Remember how we used to sing 'The Farmer in the Dell,' Dad, when I was just a little kid?"

And his father began to sing, in his old raucous voice, and Adam joined in and after a while his mother did, too, shaking her head in assumed dismay. "There isn't anyone in this car who's on key," she said, between the lines.

> *The farmer in the dell,*
> *The farmer in the dell . . .*

Later, when the rain had stopped and they were driving through Fleming, Adam said, "Suppose Mr. Grey is right and those people, whoever they are, have found out who you really are, Dad—does that mean we can't ever go back to Monument?" He thought of Amy Hertz, how he should have called her before leaving. The possibility of not ever seeing her again made him lonely.

"We've had false alarms before, Adam," his

father said. "Chances are this one is, too. Grey always looks on the dark side of things. That's what makes him so good at his job, I guess."

"Look," his mother said, "let's not talk about all that. This is supposed to be a pleasure trip. A weekend away from Monument. Let's not talk about anything gloomy . . ."

So they drove and his father recited some fragments of Thomas Wolfe, about October and the tumbling leaves of bitter red, or yellow leaves like living light, and Adam was sad again, thinking of his father as a writer and how his life had changed, how it had been necessary for him to give up all that and become another person altogether, how all of them had become other persons, his father, his mother, and himself. Paul Delmonte, poor lost Paul Delmonte.

They stopped to eat at a MacDonald's because Adam had a weakness for hamburgers and then they resumed the journey and the sun came out now and then. His father suggested that they find a motel before darkness fell and then go out to a good restaurant later. His father wasn't fond of MacDonald's and had toyed indifferently with the fish filet.

"Look," his mother said.

They looked. It wasn't really a motel but a string of cabins set back from the road with a sign near the roadway that said *Rest-A-While Motel.*

"Why not stay there," his mother asked. "It looks more romantic than those antiseptic motels."

"Right," said his father, steering the car off the

road. His father made arrangements while he and his mother stayed in the car. When his father returned, he said, "There's one big cabin that can accommodate three people—they'll bring in a cot. That way, we can stay together."

Again, that small shiver along Adam's flesh.

But they had a fine time that night. They found a restaurant called the Red Mill by a hustling brook complete with an old water wheel and his father and mother were in a good mood, his mother not so sad, a smile sometimes lingering at the corners of her lips. "Wine does this to her, makes her smile a lot," his father said, amused. Adam felt a sense of sharing. He was glad now that his father had told him all the secrets. He felt as though he were part of the family. Once, in a rush of affection, he placed his hand over his mother's hand and squeezed. She smiled—not the wine smile but her old smile of tenderness and love and contentment. He looked at his father. It was impossible to squeeze his hand, of course, not at this age. But he regarded him with warmth and affection.

Later, they made an adventure of the cabin, arranging the furniture to accommodate the cot. It reminded Adam of an old movie he'd seen on television—*It Happened One Night*, with Clark Gable and some actress, Claudette Somebody—and his father and mother remembered the movie, too, and it was good talking and joking and reminiscing, and then settling down. Adam lay awake long after his parents were asleep, listening to the night noises, listening to their breathing, his father's rhythmic snoring, his mother's fluttering breath.

The next morning, they planned to head far to the north, to Burlington and St. Albans and even farther to the Canadian border although his father said they couldn't cross the border, of course. He said that Barre was on the road north, a stonecutter's town where Italians years ago had come to work on the quarries, reminiscent of Blount, and it might be interesting to visit there. So they set out on the road to Barre, on a brilliant October morning, the leaves a riot of color. The road was a state highway but not a major interstate. Sweeping, climbing curves greeted them and majestic landscapes unfolded in the distance, with farmhouses and barns scattered here and there in the vistas.

"It would be lonely if we weren't together," his mother said.

"I think there's a car following us," his father said.

He spoke so calmly and so matter-of-factly, as if commenting on the weather or something, that the meaning of his words had no immediate impact on Adam.

"I saw it this morning, across the street from the cabin at the gas station," his father said, still cool, still calm. "Let's not panic. I'm going to slow down and pull toward the side of the road as if we want to look at the view and we'll see what happens."

Adam felt his mother stiffen.

"Who do you think it is, Dad?"

"It could be anybody at all. Somebody like us, meandering around the countryside. Or it could

be Grey's men. He likes to act the part of watchdog. For our own good, he says."

"Be careful, Dave," his mother said.

His father slowed the car at an apron of dirt at
the side of the road, not too big for parking, but
far enough off the road so that they could look out
at the countryside, farmlands in the distance, buildings like small toys.

The car that his father said had been following
them—a tan Dodge of no outstanding style—drove
leisurely by without hesitation, going neither fast
nor slow. Two men were in the front seat. They
looked straight ahead as the car passed.

Adam's father shook his head. "Grey's men," he
said, wryly. "I'd know them anywhere. Never any
privacy."

"Let's be glad it's them," his mother said.

They pushed on, the tan Dodge out of sight, and
the scenery grew more dramatic as the road
climbed. In the far distance, a mountain swept
toward the sky, its peak gleaming in the sunlight.

"Oh, David," his mother exclaimed.

They had rounded a curve and encountered a
breathtaking vista, the edge of a roadway like a
balcony looking out on miles and miles of countryside, a river below twisting like a thin black snake
through the mottled earth.

His father brought the car to a halt at the edge
of the road. "Let's stretch our legs," he said.

"I have a feeling we can see Canada," his mother
said, tossing her hand toward the distance, as they
walked toward the view.

That was when they heard the sound of a car. Fast, accelerating, whining. A sound erupting out of nowhere. Adam spun around. Not a car out of nowhere but from around a nearby curve. A car hurtling toward them, metal flashing in the sun.

The car was upon them, sickeningly.

Adam screamed. Or had his mother screamed? He turned as if to run and then turned back again and heard a scream—whose?—cut off in mid-breath. He saw—

> *(10-second interval.)*
> *A:* Nothing.
> *T:* You saw something. Of course you did.
> *A:* Yes.
> *T:* What did you see?
> *A:* The car. Like a monster. The car.
> *T:* What else?
> *A:* Nothing. Just the car.
> *T:* And what did the car do?
> *A:* A bowling ball. Like a bowling ball. Smashing. Crashing.
> *T:* Into what? Into who?
> *(10-second interval.)*
> *T:* You must say it.
> *(5-second interval.)*
> *T:* You must not stop now.
> *(6-second interval.)*
> *T:* You must not stop now.

Into them. Into his father, his mother, himself. The car smashing, shattering. A flash of steel, sun glinting, and he felt himself, crazily, moving through the air, no feeling, no pain, no sense of flight, but actually in the air, not flying but moving as if in slow motion, everything slowed down, tumbling now and twisting and in the tumbling and the twisting he saw his mother die. Instantly. Death without any doubt, and he regarded her almost curiously, numb, without feeling. One moment, she was spinning the way he was spinning, like a top released from its string, and suddenly she was actually on the hood of the car, sliding, sliding toward the windshield in that terrible kind of slow motion, and then she was sliding back toward the front of the car, as if someone had reversed the film projector, and she fell to the pavement, not sliding off but plunging to the pavement strangely, awkwardly, her head at an odd angle, almost at a right angle to her body. She stared at him with startled eyes but she was not really staring at him because Adam knew the eyes were sightless, vacant. She was dead, irrevocably dead, the knowledge irrefutable as he lay on the pavement now, his own strange flight ended somehow—he didn't know how, he didn't know when he had stopped moving in the air—and he continued to stare at her, unable to move, unable to talk, unable to do anything, and he felt all wet and oozy as if he were lying in a swamp, and he was aware of something warm and wet encompassing him as he looked at his mother, her head at that wrong angle, a rag doll tossed away.

A voice: "He got away—he's not here."

Another voice: "I saw him run. He's hurt."

Another voice: "They'll get him—they never miss."

His father—they were talking about his father. His father had to get away. He clung to the thought.

Pounding feet now, echoing on the pavement and the echoes loud because his ear was pressed to the pavement; his cheek felt bruised, lacerated, and he was still facing his mother and she was still dead, of course, her head at that peculiar angle. He did not want to look at her anymore. He lay numb, in a vacuum except for the echo of sounds in his ear and he tried to raise his head from the pavement but couldn't and he wanted to close his eyes but couldn't and he couldn't bear to look at his mother anymore. He. Did. Not. Want. To. Look. At. Her. Anymore. She. Was. Dead.

He felt a need to move, to get up, to raise himself from the pavement, to turn. He exerted all his strength, all his determination, the pavement scratching his cheek like sandpaper as he moved and he finally turned his head slightly and swiveled his eyes to see—

T: What did you see?

Him. Him. Walking toward him and his mother, tall, saw him tall, taller than ever because he looked tallest of all from the pavement, and his mouth was moving as he came, walking, walking . . .

T: Tell me. It's important.

Coming closer, looming, closer still, his legs like a giant's legs, like someone on stilts maybe, and hearing the words coming from his mouth now: "He'll never get away." But he will, his father had to get away. The legs moved toward his mother and the mouth spoke: "She's terminated." Hearing the words and not wanting to hear them. Seeing him come closer, the legs walking toward him again, hovering over him now.

T: Who did you see?

Gray pants. Him. Hearing his voice again: "Move fast. Remove her. The boy—check him. He may be useful. Fast now, fast."

Hands grappled his body but there was still no pain, and a sudden weariness engulfed him, a sweet and delicious weariness enveloped him, caressed him, and he gave himself up to it, his face heavy now and his eyes heavy, and the weariness was beautiful, taking him, gathering him. His eyes fluttered like his mother's breath had fluttered long ago and he rose up to the weariness and then settled down into it, soft and gentle and tender . . .

T: Who? Who?
(5-second interval.)

T :   You must not retreat now.
         (5-second interval.)
T :   You must not withdraw.
         (5-second interval.)
T :   Can you respond? Are you able to respond?
         (5-second interval.)
T :   Lift your hand if you can respond.
         (30 second interval.)
T :   Let the record show: no response.

END TAPE OZK015

———————

I turn the corner and I'm in Rutterburg.

I pedal along, refreshed and at ease in the cool of morning.

Rutterburg is deserted, not a soul in sight, as if everyone has been wiped out by a science-fiction holocaust.

I pedal smoothly, my arms and legs moving beautifully, coordinated, and it seems as if pedaling the bike is second nature now, part of my existence, something I was born to do.

I look for a telephone booth but I don't see any. I'm not sure why I want to find a phone booth; in fact, the thought of a phone booth makes me sad. I don't know why it makes me sad but it does. It opens up a loneliness in me, like a hole, a deep, dark hole. The hole is threatening somehow; if it gets too big it could swallow me up, so I try not to think about it. The medicine always helps me not to think about it.

I turn the corner and see the hospital. The iron gates gleam in the sun; they were recently painted a hideous orange but Dr. Dupont says this is only the undercoating, the gates will be painted black again later. I pedal toward the gates and I am glad to be back. My legs are getting stiff now and my fingers are numb. I reach the gates and Dr. Dupont is waiting for me. He is always waiting for me. He is a big man with white hair and a sad black mustache and his voice is always soft, always gentle.

"Well, you're here," he says, and he is glad to see me. I get off the bike with a flourish to show him how expert I am.

I glance outside through the gates. Someday I will ride my bike out there.

"I didn't take the medicine, Doctor," I tell him. It is very cold now and my body begins to tremble. He places his arm around my shoulder.

"That's all right," he murmurs.

I push my bike along the path that leads to the hospital and he walks along beside me. The hospital is on a small hill in front of us, a white building with black shutters and columns in front, like a southern mansion.

"Welcome back, Skipper," someone calls. I look up to see Mr. Harvester, the old maintenance man. His voice is loud and he smiles at me and I smile back. He mows the lawn and does odd jobs and he is always planning trips somewhere, reading books and maps and travel magazines. But he never goes anywhere. The red veins in his face resemble the road maps he's always reading.

The doctor and I continue to walk and I am tired suddenly. All that riding.

"Well, what do you know—the traveler's back," Whipper says. He is sitting on the porch with his two friends, Dobbie and Lewis. They are wise guys. I don't look at them. They are always playing pranks. Once when I was riding the bike around the grounds—Dr. Dupont allows me to do this if I promise not to leave the place—Whipper and his friends chased me and knocked me off and I went flying into a ditch. Whipper is staring at me as I go by and there's a smirk on his face. I don't look at him but I know the smirk is there. He's always trying to steal my box from me. As we go by Whipper, I clutch the box tightly.

Inside, the smell of lilac fills the hallway as usual. Dr. Dupont tries to keep the place homelike. "This is not an institution but a home, a haven for troubled people," he says.

I hear a growl as we proceed down the hall. I am tired, as if I have not slept for a long time, and when I hear the growl of the dog, I am almost too tired to be afraid.

"Now, now," Dr. Dupont says, "everything's all right." He calls into the other room: "Get Silver out of here—I told you to keep him outdoors."

Silver is a German shepherd and he is ferocious. He delights in chasing people and knocking them down. He chases me whenever I ride my bike.

We pass the office at the end of the hallway where Luke, the switchboard operator, is usually stationed. Sometimes, Luke helps to serve the meals and he often gives me extra portions to build me up physically. I wave to him as we pass and he waves back, nodding his head, the mouthpiece clamped to his chin.

Dr. Dupont and I climb the stairs, and Arthur Haynes leans over, watching our progress up the spiral staircase. Arthur Haynes is big and fat and always perspiring. He does not say anything but watches us go up and he looks sad. He is always scratching himself. He gives me the creeps. Arthur Haynes always stays on the second floor, behind the banister, and his eyes follow everybody. I try not to let my eyes meet his.

We reach the top of the stairs and begin walking toward my room and although I do not like it here and I feel somehow that I do not belong here, there is a feeling of belonging, of being among familiar things. I know that Junior Varney lurks somewhere and will try to steal my bike. I know the bad times in the night. I know about that room where they will ask me questions. But I am tired and I am glad my room is waiting.

My room is small and comfortable, with blue wallpaper, gold birds flying on the blue. Dr. Dupont goes to my bureau and returns with the medicine. I swallow the two pills and drink the water.

I sit in the chair and look at the window. Frost edges the windowpane.

"My father," I say, looking at the window. There are no bars on the window, not like that other room where I sit and answer questions. I hope I don't have to go there anymore. "Is my father dead?" I ask.

"Please," Dr. Dupont says, "relax now. Let the medicine do its work. Then we'll talk." His voice is soothing, like syrup, not like that other voice in that other room. I don't want to think about that other room. But I keep thinking about my father.

"My father is dead, isn't he?" I ask. I know that my mother is dead. I have knowledge that she is dead. I don't know how I know but I do. But my father is different. I wonder if he is out there somewhere, waiting for me to find him. I wonder if he is out there somewhere, hurt, injured, waiting for me to bring him help.

"We are all mortal," Dr. Dupont says, his voice gentle. "We must all die someday." His voice is so gentle that I lean back in the chair.

"My poor father," I say. "He is dead, isn't he? He didn't get away, did he?"

The doctor's face is sad; his face is always sad

when we talk about my father and I find out again that he is dead.

The doctor takes the package from my hand and I begin to sing:

> *The farmer in the dell,*
> *The farmer in the dell,*
> *Heigh-ho, the merry-o,*
> *The farmer in the dell* . . .

It makes me feel good when I sing. I watch Dr. Dupont as I sing. He is opening the box. He is a kind man. The medicine is working now and I can feel it in my veins. It's singing in my veins along with me:

> *The child takes the cat,*
> *The child takes the cat,*
> *Heigh-ho, the merry-o,*
> *The child takes the cat* . . .

I am singing fine now because I know that I don't have to go into that room and answer the questions. Maybe later, of course, but not now at least.

> *The cat takes the rat,*
> *The cat takes the rat,*
> *Heigh-ho, the merry-o,*
> *The cat takes the rat* . . .

The doctor opens the box and takes out Pokey the Pig. My old friend. The doctor is a good man and he found Pokey the Pig for me. He went away and found it and also found my father's old army jacket and his old hat.

He places Pokey the Pig in my arms.

The rat takes the cheese,
The rat takes the cheese,
Heigh-ho, the merry-o,
The rat takes the cheese . . .

I rock Pokey in my arms and I'm wearing my father's jacket and I have on his old cap and now I'm not so sad anymore although I know he's dead and my mother's dead, too.

I keep singing, I keep singing.

The cheese stands alone,
The cheese stands alone,
Heigh-ho, the merry-o,
The cheese stands alone.

"Rest awhile," Dr. Dupont says. "Everything's going to be all right, Paul."

I wonder who the doctor is talking to, this somebody he calls Paul. Who is Paul? I know I am not Paul. There is another name I know about but I can't think of the name now and anyway I am too busy singing, and I hold Pokey the Pig close to me and I smile as I sing because I know, of course, who I am, who I will always be.

I am the cheese.

TAPE OZK016   1655   date deleted T

T: Annual report on File Data 865–01. Special
references: Subject A; Personnel ⌗2222;
Agency Basic Procedures.
As evidenced in attached tapes (OZK
Series), it was impossible to elicit from
Subject A information sought by
Department 1-R. Inducement of medication
(Refer: Medical Unit Group) plus

preknowledge interrogation failed to bring
forth suspected knowledge of Subject A.
Psychiatric reports (Refer: Psychiatric
Profiles Plus Analyses) corroborate results
of OZK series tapes. Subject A responded
with consistency of earlier sessions. (Refer:
Department B-2 Tape Series ORT, UDW.)
Data provided by Subject A also consistent
with earlier reactions. Deep withdrawal
when topics which concern Department 1-R
are approached. (Refer: Witness Re-
Establishment Project, File Data 865–01,
Witness ⁑599–6.) Results of questioning:
negative. (Refer: negative results in Tape
Series ORT, UDW.)

SUMMARY:
This is the third annual questioning of
Subject A with results identical to two
earlier sessions at twelve-month intervals.
Subject A discloses no awareness of data
provided Department 1-R by Witness
⁑599–6. Complete withdrawal accompanies
recapitulation of termination of Witness
⁑599–6 and affiliate (spouse). Knowledge,
however, may be psychological residue
within Subject A.

ADVISORY:
Department B-2 holds no authority under
Input For Recommendations and functions
as Advisory. The following advisories are
advanced for priority study:

Advisory ＃1:
Modification of Agency Basic Procedures
to eliminate Policy 979 which does not
currently allow termination procedures by
Department 1-R.

Advisory ＃2:
Discontinue suspension of Personnel ＃2222
and grant full reinstatement on following
basis: While it is fact that Witness ＃599–6
had been located by Adversaries, it has not
been established that Personnel ＃2222
allowed termination of Witness ＃599–6 and
affiliate (spouse) by Adversaries. (There is
only circumstancial evidence that Personnel
＃2222 contacted Adversaries regarding
location of Witness ＃599–6.) Note that
Personnel ＃2222 directed Post-Termination
activity with efficiency and dispatch as
follows: (a) Pursuit and confirmation of
Witness ＃599–6 termination by
Adversaries; (b) removal of affiliate's
remains from scene; (c) transfer of Subject
A to confinement facilities. All activities
completed without involvement of local
authorities. Third-year mandatory review
indicates Personnel ＃2222 acted within
existing policies of Agency Basic Procedures.

Advisory ＃3:
Since Subject A is final linkage between
Witness ＃599–6 and File Data 865–01, it is
advised that (a) pending revision of Agency
Basic Procedures (Refer: Policy 979) Subject

A's confinement be continued until
termination procedures are approved; or
(b) Subject A's condition be sustained until
Subject A obliterates.

END TAPE SERIES OZK016

I am riding the bicycle and I am on Route 31 in Monument, Massachusetts, on my way to Rutterburg, Vermont, and I'm pedaling furiously because this is an old-fashioned bike, no speeds, no fenders, only the warped tires and the brakes that don't always work and the handlebars with cracked rubber grips to steer with. A plain bike—the kind my father rode as a kid years ago. It's cold as I pedal along, the wind like a snake slithering up my sleeves and into my jacket and my pants legs, too. But I keep pedaling, I keep pedaling. . . .

Robert Cormier began his career as a newspaperman twenty-five years ago and since then has been involved in all phases of journalism. He is the author of three adult novels, and his first book for young adults, THE CHOCOLATE WAR, received the highest praise from critics around the country in addition to being chosen a *New York Times* Outstanding Book of the Year 1974, a Kirkus Choice, a Maxi Award winner, and an American Library Association Best Book for Young Adults, 1974. An award-winning journalist, Mr. Cormier currently writes editorials for the Fitchburg, Massachusetts, *Sentinel*.